On Unnatural Authority

Written, Edited, and Published by Alexandra Salyga Reynolds
ISBN: 978-1-7751864-1-0
London, Ontario
©2017

Table of Contents

On Unnatural Authority

Part I
Chapter 1

I lay down with my laptop under a tree. The wind faintly rustled above me and I turned my laptop to shield my screen from flying debris. I had successfully defended my thesis a week ago and still had something left to finish. The balmy air, dry ground, and screen glare-killing shade welcomed me to work outside.

The hero of my own work, I opened my manuscript to give it a final polish. In a few more weeks it was going to be published, a deadline that I was well prepared to meet.

I started at the beginning, one final run through to make sure it makes sense and be sure that nothing else needed to be changed. *If only I were detached enough to let this pass cleanly across my mind.* I knew full well my wish could never come true. The story began simply enough:

Victoria Falls rummaged through the attic. Mouldy-smelling dust kicked up as she opened a cardboard box to sort out what was ruined from what was still usable. It had only been a week since her father's funeral. He had died of cancer at seventy-nine, and now Victoria and her family were in the middle of putting his house in order for sale. Victoria had been scouring the attic for valuables and keepsakes when she discovered the water damage. Apparently the roof had sprung a leak when Thomas was occupied with his illness and needed to be repaired.

The damage was slight and contained to the roof directly above the box Victoria had just opened. Victoria sifted through the contents of the box. Almost everything was ruined; everything except an ancient, leather-bound black book, which was inexplicably undamaged. Victoria ran her hands across the leather, and fiddled with the buckle that held it shut for a moment before opening it.

The pages were made of supple vellum, and the ink was a deep, rusty red. Victoria glanced at the pages. It wasn't written in a language she could read, so she flipped for illustrations to glean what it was about. Arcane circles and charts flipped past her vision, a confusion compounded with disgust at the graphic and visceral images the book contained. Victoria settled on a page. She had come to an illustration of something she recognized. It was one of a vampire.

The figure looked like the other anatomical drawings in the book. There was a note on the end of an arrow pointed towards its heart. Victoria recognized one of the words, *cordem*.

Heart? Victoria thought. She read the note it was a part of more closely, it read: "Interfice palo in cordem". *Knowing what I know, it must mean something like 'kill with a stake to the heart'.* Victoria looked over the rest of the notes attached to the illustration. The text was definitely in Latin.

With one mystery solved, Victoria closed the book and got up to go downstairs. As she was about to leave the attic, she shoved the ruined items, mostly old magazines and newspaper clippings, back into the warped cardboard box whence they came. Victoria chuckled to herself a bit.

Victoria stopped cold when she noticed the attic floor under the box. She moved it over, "Shit!" Victoria called down the ladder, "You have to come up here and see this!"

Miles climbed up to check it out. "Look here," said Victoria, "right under the leak in the roof, this part of the floor that the warped cardboard box over there was sitting on has rotted."

Miles leaned over the spot, "It isn't completely rotted through; that box must have been sitting there moist for some time, to let this much mold eat at Tommy's attic."

"Damn," went Miles, "there's no telling how far it's spread from here without ripping up the floor. At least all the beams directly involved and those touching them need to be replaced, maybe more if the mold's spread."

"This is going to cost us a lot of money," Victoria shook her head. "And to think that we were under the impression that handling my father's estate as legitimately as possible would help us avoid problems."

"It already has," responded Miles. "I got an email in my executor identity's box from Captain Daylight. They passed us over as the source of the suspicious deaths around here. Our wonderful superhero-secret-identity vampire hunter thinks we're just the hired executors of the will of an old man who died without any family. He still found it necessary to tell me I'd been passed over." Miles showed the barest hint of anger, and Victoria picked up on the mood.

"Fuck Captain Daylight. That anyone could consider him, her, or it, a hero," her voice sputtered out before she got herself together to speak again. It rankled her that someone like that, who had killed anywhere between fifteen and forty-seven, of her kind, hid themself so well. Victoria's voice returned, "It hunts us down mercilessly. Serious, Nazi-level persecution."

"I wouldn't go so far." Miles' wife had followed the voices into the attic: "I heard from my friend, you know the one who lives off the blood drained from the embalming process." The other two nodded to show they knew who she was talking about.

Victoria felt a faint shudder of disgust. Miles directed his focus on where Ara was going with this. "Well she told me that she'd gotten a visit from Captain Daylight, who spared her after she had proven that she never killed humans to feed. Mara said she had sworn not to reveal anything about his identity, not his gender, or appearance, or anything."

Ara sighed before continuing. "I doubt Mara would have been very helpful even if she didn't feel bound by her word. Her diet of dead blood has taken a severe toll on her. Death has infected her, and she has lost many of her mental faculties." Ara sunk into silent contemplation for a moment before pulling herself forcibly to the present:

"What's wrong with the attic, then?"

"Victoria found some water damage with mold under the leak in the roof." Miles punctuated his remark with a gesture to the spot on the floor.

Ara sunk back into her grief over the world's decay. Victoria suppressed the urge to roll her eyes. As vampires, endless life is here for us to enjoy, we can know all of history until the sun expands and burns the Earth to cinders. We could even leave it in time to live on another world. *Yet my friend and adopted mother wallows in a perverse attraction to death and decay*. Victoria could not comprehend her mindset.

Miles and Ara went downstairs to find and get ahold of a contractor to fix the attic. Victoria started to load up the truck with boxes of stuff for the dump. When she got back Miles and Ara had already made the arrangements for fixing the attic for sale. "It'll definitely be expensive," Miles told her.

Victoria returned to the attic to start loading up the useable items they didn't need to give away. Victoria carried the disturbing black book tucked into her hoodie's front pocket, where she'd put it unconsciously while she called Miles to the attic.

As Victoria adjusted her grip on a particularly ungainly piece of furniture she was moving to truck bed, Victoria noticed the book for the first time since she put it in her pocket. Victoria put the tall, skinny bookshelf down in the truck and took out the book. Out in the overcast day, the book looked much less impressive than it had inside under the light of the attic's single dangling bulb.

Its black leather cover was scuffed and its colour had faded along the spine, as if the book had spent a long time sitting on a shelf exposed to direct sunlight. Opening it up, Victoria now saw that the vellum pages were yellowed with age, and that what had seemed to be dark red ink inside was in fact mostly faded sepia, with chapter titles and emphasized words done in black. How Victoria had smooshed the two colours together in her head the first time eluded her.

The Latin writing was mixed with snippets of many other languages. Victoria could make out the German bits well enough, but the book was mostly in Latin. If she came across a werewolf she knew how to identify it in its human form and nothing else, since that piece of information was quoted in German, but the rest of the section was unreadable in Latin.

Looking up to see that it had started to get dark during her examination, Victoria put the book back in her pocket and got back onto her task. On the way back, Victoria stopped by the University bookstore and bought an introductory Latin textbook. She had her next project.

Ara, Miles and Victoria returned to their home when they had done all they could at Thomas' house. It was a nondescript-looking place in a suburb near Vancouver. If anyone had asked, they would have said that Victoria and her companions of an apparently similar age were students renting rooms from Miles and Ara.

Life continued more or less like it had before Victoria's father died. Victoria got into her Latin study: she sat down by her window with the textbook.

Hours later, Victoria turned from her book to the sound of her door opening and closing. Valentin was standing in the middle of her room, "Darling," he started, "Mother Ara wants you downstairs."

"Is anything happening?" Victoria shut the book.

"Something is happening with Captain Daylight," Valentin said, "Ara found a press release from them online, and we need to discuss it."

"What did it tell the internet?"

Valentin shrugged, "Ara has it on her computer, you'll see it downstairs." Victoria got up and followed him downstairs to where the rest of her coven's members were gathered in a clump in the TV room.

Ara passed her laptop with the online announcement open to Victoria and Valentin. Valentin held the device so they could both read it. The announcement took the form of a prepared statement released on a somewhat well-known paranormal blogger's website.

Anna Carlson, the blogger, introduced Captain Daylight's press release with a long disclaimer of knowledge of the vampire hunter's identity. She went so far as to post a screenshot of the email she received from Captain Daylight that contained the statement to prove that she had never met them. The statement was nicely typed out beneath the screenshot, even though it was visible in the email.

After Valentin had finished with the laptop, Victoria had it to herself. She read the post over again:

> To all those whom my fame has reached,
> I have dedicated my life to the protection of humanity from monsters. Until now, I have succeeded in preserving both my own and others' human lives from the depredation of vampires. As recent events have shown me, I am, despite being humanity's greatest warrior against evil, still very much mortal. To defend against the death of my techniques for killing vampires along with me, I have selected several people to train. They will carry on the defense of humanity after I have gone, either in carrying out my duty or from nature's course, so my death will be no salvation for vampirekind.
>
> Vampires,
> Your days of stalking the night with nothing but each other to fear are over. Human beings will not be to you as cattle are to them. We will not be your food. We will not be fought over in secret wars. We will not die to prolong your lives. Either stop killing humans or die.

Humans,

      Most of you live under the belief that vampires are not real. You may believe that the deluded only believe themselves to be vampires. You may only be swayed by concrete and authoritative proof of their existence. For you skeptics I offer video proof. I have in my sights an active coven of vampires in the Pacific Northwest of North America. Within two weeks, I will publish a video proving the inhuman strength and endurance of the vampire as I kill off the members of this coven. I cannot unduly warn my target, so that is all the information I may give you now.

The blogger finished her post with a few paragraphs of moral inquietude over what amounted to Captain Daylight announcing the publication of a snuff film. She went on about how this had dampened her admiration of them. Victoria got the gist and skimmed down to the comments to the blog post. It was, predictably, full of arguments about the Captain's gender and the ethics of filming death for proof. There was little talk of doubting the existence of vampires, which was not a surprise given Carlson's audience.

What was a surprise was the amount of controversy over the specifics of what Captain Daylight had announced. Victoria glared at comments from assholes arguing about how and where the videos will be shot and what vampire-fighting techniques Captain Daylight will reveal. The commentators suggested and sniped at various major and minor cities as potential locations, but Victoria's concern was if it was talking about herself and the others.

The comments wore Victoria down. The sound of her closest friends worried for their lives grated against the detached speculation of strangers who didn't expect to ever meet those whose fate they discussed. They'd just watch them die and argue over whether the video is fake or not. *Am I a part of the target or aren't I?* Victoria fumed at the commentators' attitude.

Miles knew of several nearby covens in Vancouver and the environs. Ara knew some, too. Valentin contributed a coven in Washington state, "did Northern California count as Pacific Northwest? They're right by the Oregon border," He added. No one knew. They moved on.

Victoria herself contributed a coven in Alaska, which she prefaced with its unlikelihood of being the one, "when I knew them, Cara and Lille were dedicated to living off of animals. That's why they moved to the Alaskan wilderness."

"This Captain Daylight might not be the one who spared Mara," Ara told the group.

"Yes," continued Miles, "there might be dozens of hunters wearing the Captain Daylight hat."

"The kills do make more sense if there are more than one of them," Victoria added, "and now the damn thing's own press release confirms it. Before we only had suspicious distances that cast doubt on the legitimacy of Captain Daylight's claims to kills."

She noticed movement beside her but kept going, "I've talked to Miles about this; I found it suspicious that Captain Daylight claimed to have killed Claudius in Mexico and Camilla in the UK, both impressive fighters, in the same week. One week, two notoriously strong vampires, one suspicious claim." Victoria sank back into her own thoughts.

"I think we were more or less agreed that Captain Daylight was more than one person," Ara responded, "the more important issue now is how we can best preserve ourselves."

"Of course," Victoria fell silent. Richard spoke next:

"We may or may not be the target. There are a few hundred vampires split into dozens of covens in the Pacific Northwest. Even if you define it as narrowly as possible, that still leaves more than a dozen covens with about a hundred members." He glanced around his audience for a moment, briefly flustered by what he had to say, "We do have peripheral contact with Daylight through Mara, but in her state..."

"God knows what she did or didn't tell 'em, or which Captain Daylight she spoke to." Ira filled in, "If she did reveal details about us, she may have muddled them enough to make them useless, putting our names on another coven, or named an old location, or messed up our contact details some other way."

"I don't think she'd be any help for information leading to us was my point," Richard finished.

"It doesn't matter," everyone turned towards Miles' voice, "they either will or won't target us, but someone close to us, a friend or an acquaintance, will definitely die for this demonstration." Miles' voice suddenly cut off. He pulled himself together. Ira shifted her weight from leg to leg as she waited impatiently for Miles to finish speaking.

"No matter who Captain Daylight targets," Miles sighed, "It's bad for us. They will disseminate vampire-killing techniques to humans who won't follow their ethics. We will face more danger from hunters. Even if they're all inexperienced and acting out what they saw online, their numbers and the exposure their attempts will draw will harm our cover." A heavy silence followed his speech.

Ara broke it, "We should brush up on our self-defense skills; we need to be prepared if they come." The tension diffused as they moved on to the practicalities of arranging for a few sessions of secret fighting practice. It was a much more fruitful conversation. In a few hours, they had a plan.

Chapter 2

Victoria and her covenmates went to the place in the Rockies they'd chosen to practice. The trees reached into the sky and gripped deeply into the mountainside. The group hiked up to a small terrace ringed by dangerously inclined slopes and paired off to practice.

Victoria first sparred with Ara, then each of the others in turn. She shifted techniques for each opponent: all the better to be prepared for whatever Captain Daylight would bring to bear against us, all the better to stave off boredom. *If we ever meet it and fall, no one could say that we didn't at least try to save ourselves.*

"You know what," said Victoria after they'd been through a round of sparring everyone, "we should take it up a notch." She sat down on the ground where the others were gathering to rest and continued, "we should try and learn how to fight from a height. It's always better to use our inhuman strength."

"That's a logical extension of what we've been doing here," said Miles, "you and Richard have already taken to working off the trees. Show us something." Victoria and Richard got up and distanced themselves from the group. The others turned to face them.

"Why did you have to volunteer us?" Richard whispered at her.

Victoria sneered at him as they continued to walk away from the group, "It's as if you want us to die without having done all we can to preserve ourselves. Because there is precious little in this life we can control for ourselves, not how our enemies will attack us, not if we will be targeted now or ever, but only our own resources to respond to them better."

"You pretentious dick," Richard hissed, "this exercise is pointless; it only soothes your paranoia. We won't be chosen." We turned to face each other. He looked pissed and I arched an eyebrow at him.

"Then you'll have a new useless skill." Richard cut Victoria off by starting the demonstration. Victoria stepped away from his rush and swung him past her into the trees. Richard latched onto the tree he hit and scrambled up to a branch, while Victoria rushed towards the base of the same tree.

Richard bounced off his branch to spike down onto Victoria, who once again deflected him. This time she plucked him out of the air and flung him down onto the slope.

Victoria hit the ground at the base of the tree; Richard dug into the mountainside to stop his descent. Victoria climbed the tree and performed the manoeuver that Richard had just attempted on her. She got him moments after he regained a stable footing and pinned him down at the base of another tree. "It's lucky that we didn't end up sliding down the mountain in earnest. This is not at all intentional."

Richard glared at Victoria in response.

"Come back," called Miles, "and have a rest. We have what we need for now."

Richard and Victoria sat down on opposite sides of the group, which fell into a discussion of the possible uses for what they'd seen. Valentin turned to Victoria and said, "I suppose that we could use this in the city with buildings and lampposts and whatever else, but we're deeply hampered by a lack of a sufficiently secret urban practice area."

"We really should look for somewhere," Victoria replied, "It'll give us an advantage against our enemies."

Ara spoke over Valentin to Victoria, "I know of somewhere abandoned that we might take over for a few days." Richard continued to grumble about the bother of training. Ira and Miles didn't approve of his lassitude, and Valentin and Victoria joined their side against him. Ara quieted them down.

The rest of the training trip passed without further drama. Richard was sullen and gloomy, but went along with what everyone else was doing. As the discussions during the breaks got more and more perfunct, Victoria spent more and more of the break time working on her Latin.

They came back down the mountain a fortnight after they went up it. As they loaded back into the car, Victoria decided that she had gotten far enough with the language to get into the book she left back home.

The coven dispersed across the house when they got back. Victoria went straight to her room and took the mysterious book out from the box filled with packing peanuts where she'd instinctively hidden it. She brushed the crumbled remains of the peanuts off the cover.

Victoria sat down, transfixed by the book. She read the title, *De Innaturale Potestate*. "It's time to acquire some unnatural power." The open cover extended itself behind Victoria's notice, grasping her tightly by the mind.

Victoria jerked back to the present. Ira had grabbed her shoulder to get her attention. She pushed the sides of the book together and turned her attention to Ira. "Goddamn it, you've been stuck here for six weeks. Put that all the way down. Seriously. All the way into the box; and close the box. Completely. Something has happened."

Ira stepped away to lead her downstairs, but turned back on her heels when she didn't hear Victoria following her. Victoria was motionless in her chair, facing the corner to the right of Ira with a vacant stare. "Victoria, get your head out of your obsession. Captain Daylight has posted a snuff film. Come see it," Ira followed her statement with a withering glare.

Victoria rubbed her face. "How long have I been here?"

"I just told you. As soon as we got down from the mountain you sat down with that creepy book and haven't moved for six weeks."

"Six weeks?" Victoria pulled herself up from her seat.

"Yes, six weeks. You could've at least moved around a bit once and awhile. You've fucked yourself up; all that fitness from the trip," she made a swift gesture, "Fwoosh, gone."

Victoria shuffled to the middle of the room, "Has anything happened about Captain Daylight?"

Ira snorted, "Come watch the video." Ira led the way downstairs, and this time Victoria followed. Victoria searched herself for what she'd been reading for so long, but couldn't find anything where the memory should have been. It tugged gently at her attention. As Victoria slowly pulled herself into the moment, the blackout solidified into a concrete mass over what happened. Ira kept talking, "I've never seen you so obsessed, I should really take a look at that book."

"Nah," was Victoria's response, "It's a fairly ordinary, yet accurate, sixteenth-century monster compendium. In Latin. You'll only bore yourself with it."

"Great to see you're all the way back." They reached the others to see that they had gathered around the shared PC. Valentin was scrolling through the comments under a video and reading them out for metacommentary.

"Here's another asshole who thinks that the vampire's purple blood is CGI," called Valentin. Ira snorted. Valentin noticed Victoria was there.

"Miles and Ara have had enough of it," he said, "so it's just us here to show you the video." Valentin scrolled up to the top of the page and replayed the video.

Victoria sat down in the chair and Valentin hovered over her shoulder. She stared at the screen as the video began. The picture shook over a poorly-lit parking lot as the camera was set down. The camera's autofocus shifted from the lot to the figure that stepped into frame from behind the camera. A dim glow shone from a blade peeking from in front of the figure's billowing coat as whoever-it-was walked out into the open.

The figure went out of focus as another darted out into the open. It was a pale man in scruffy clothes who came out of the brush at the edge of the parking lot. The autofocus had latched onto him. Seeing the person who had set the camera down, and hedged in by a ring of masked hunters that came out of the bushes, he stood to fight. Victoria stared intently at the vampire's face as it came in and out of focus at the whim of the cheap camera's autofocus. It was all Victoria could manage not to start screaming in frustration as she struggled to identify the hunted vampire.

"It's Michael Burgher," Victoria shouted, "I know him from that marathon screening. He lives in that terrible small town in Oregon, the one I said looked like the town from *Twin Peaks*. Or lived, shit."

The video went on to show Michael defend himself against six hunters, four of whom kept him trapped in the parking lot and two of whom engaged him in close combat. They wielded glowing blades with unremarkable technique. Victoria glared at the lethal edges, demanding they give up their secrets. The video ended when one from the outer line turned off the camera. Michael had been killed and the glowing material of the hunters' weapons remained unknown.

Victoria fumed for a moment before refreshing the page for the newest comments: "He was more than six hundred years old." The page refreshed to an error message. Apparently the site was down.

"God knows when or if it'll be back up again," Ira griped.

Victoria listened to the others' summary of the comments as they were. They had speculated on what the glowing material was, where the video was shot, who was in the hunting party, why the vampire was unable to escape the hunters, and above all whether the whole thing was fake. Valentin did most of the summarizing, with occasional tidbits from Ira and Richard.

Once they were done, Victoria refreshed the page to the same error message. Recognizing defeat, at least for the moment, Victoria got up from the computer. She told the others, "Now that I can't do anything else with this video, I'll be out to feed."

"Thanks for the broadcast," Ira's sarcasm followed Victoria out the door. Victoria wandered the neighbourhood for a bit before latching onto a target. A suspicious rapping sound from a fist knocking on a windowpane reached her. Victoria followed it to a basement window facing the backyard of a house two blocks away from hers. A woman looked out at her. She shouted through the glass, "I'm kidnapped. Get me out of here. A serial killer's gonna be back here soon."

Victoria broke the glass between them and pulled out the shards still attached to the frame. It had been sealed from opening normally with extra wood framing and a mess of caulk. Victoria pulled her out through the opening, noticing that she had lost three of her fingers to her captor. Victoria handed her the cell phone from her pocket and told her to call for medical attention. The killer was in the house.

He had heard the glass breaking, and had picked up his cattle prod before entering the holding cell in his basement. Victoria hopped down into the completely empty room through the glassless window. There were only one blanket, one knobless door, and smooth, plastered-over walls in the entire room. The killer finished with the locks and got in, lunging at what he thought was his escaping captive and brandishing the cattle prod.

Victoria met him instead. She incapacitated him in an instant by breaking his brandishing arm and set to feeding. The killer was dead in less than five minutes. Victoria quickly darted through the rest of the house, claiming a few choice valuables left lying in plain sight from the house before the authorities arrived.

She left late enough to hear the victim telling someone official that her rescuer had gone into the house and she had heard a fight. Victoria didn't linger. Cash jar cradled close, she rushed home by way of an undeveloped gulley that cut through the neighbourhood. Victoria skirted the stream that flowed at the bottom and entered the coven house's lot through the back gate.

Victoria went in through the storm door into the basement and washed off in the dedicated post-kill shower. Upstairs again, she put the jar of cash on the counter and announced to the room, "I hit the jackpot. I got to eat a serial killer, free his victim, and rob the serial killer all in one outing. There has to be at least a thousand bucks in here. Serves him right for leaving it above the fridge where anyone can see it."

Ira snorted from the sofa in the adjoining TV room. "What a terrible, showboating thing to do right when we need to lay low. I really hate you sometimes." Ira turned towards Victoria on the sofa, "I could hear the sirens, it must have been close. Where was this cash hoarder?"

"Very conveniently located. His house backs onto the back gulley like ours." Victoria preempted Ira's obvious objection, "Yes, I know how easily the cops can track me back here. I also know how inaccurately my dear rescue described me."

Victoria heard Ira's strangled gargle of frustration, "You know how much I hate this confused witness ploy. It's a paper shield. It only works when the authorities respect their duty to the law enough to follow the trail to its end, find us, be unable to match any of us to the witness' description and accept that a) this isn't sufficient proof to bring legitimate consequences to bear against us and b) they are obliged not to bring down extralegal consequences. I hate to depend on anyone else's moral sensibilities for survival. Remember what happened the last time one of us went to jail? I thought so." Ira left without another word.

As if it had been called for Victoria's convenience, it rained for the rest of the night. The next morning, local news reported that nothing solid was known of the vigilante that had killed during the previous night. She had fled the scene and the only witness could provide a sketchy and vague description. The police searched the gulley behind the crime scene extremely slowly due to safety concerns about searching it in the dark. The heavy rain in the wee hours of the morning put a stop to the search and obliterated whatever evidence may have remained. In the subsequent investigation, five tortured bodies were found buried in the backyard. It seems someone was on Victoria's side, shielding her from harm as a consequence of killing that serial killer.

Anna turned away from her laptop. That paragraph seemed a bit bloated. As she considered how to edit it down, the wind picked up and it started to threaten rain. She shut her laptop and brought it inside the Social Sciences Centre. She set herself back up in the anteroom that passed for her office. "Hey Anna," another grad student had spoken to her.

"Hey," responded Anna. Try though she might, Anna could not recall the name of this hipsterish guy. She remembered seeing him at her thesis presentation and in the mandatory research seminar course, and that he was studying how Catholicism and traditional beliefs have affected each other and their practitioners among one of the First Nations around here. Anna remembered how he had joked about the convenience for interviews, but neither his name nor the name of the tribe he studied.

"I thought you were done writing," he continued.

"I am. This isn't my thesis," she responded, "How's yours gone?"

"Ugh, I fucked up with a bit of paperwork. I need to bring the right piece of paper from the ethics committee to the Grad Chair to say that I obeyed the rules with how I treated my subjects." The other student shifted his weight between his feet. "Have you seen him? I need to give the Chair the paper that says that no interviewees were harmed in the making of this thesis."

"I just got here; his office has definitely been empty for the last five minutes. I couldn't guess where he is now."

Forgethisname kept talking, "How did it go for you getting research ethics clearance for human subjects for your project?"

Anna shrugged, "Mine is less politically loaded than yours. I just filled out the forms they told me to and other people did most of the work." Internally, she was getting impatient. *I want to get back to my work, not make fake comradely chatter with some asshole I barely spoke to over the four years we'd both been in the program.* "The real life vampire subculture I studied is nice and safe from that point of view."

Something on her face must have made him get the point that he was unwelcome, so he ducked out to come again later. Anna made a point to be gone by the time he got back. She did not need this loser pathetically mooning over her right before she left school. *He had wasted four years too uncommitted to ask me out, or maybe less than that, I wouldn't know.*

Anna resettled in one of the study booths on the fourth floor. Rain splattered on the skylight above the main staircase. Anna fixed the wrap-up to the section on Victoria's killing of the serial killer Dennis Quaite.

As if at the behest of a benevolent supernatural power, an unexpected rainstorm in the wee hours of the morning after the death of the serial killer, named on the news as Dennis Quaite, halted the police search of the ravine and washed away Victoria's trail. They eventually found the bodies of five other tortured victims buried in his backyard under some landscape features Quaite had added over the ten years he had lived in the house. Shauna Arbour, who had been rescued by Victoria Falls, was only able to give a vague account of Victoria, saying only that she was white, unusually strong for her size, had dark hair and wore a black hoodie. The cell phone she gave to call for help with was a prepay burner phone that led nowhere.

Victoria was pleased with her escape. Every day brought her more news of her meal's crimes. It gave her no end of smug satisfaction to have taken out a serial killer that used his position as a social worker to get to people that wouldn't be missed. What was lost on her were the parallels between his and her own usual habits of hunting human beings.

Business went on as usual for a few months at the coven's house. Victoria continued to study the mysterious book. She took chunks of time, about a week per session, and sat with it. Victoria put some serious thought into which ancient language to learn next so that she could access more of the book's secrets, and while all this went on, she followed Captain Daylight's broadcast vampire kills. Ira captured each video, including the first, from the site so they could keep a copy despite the illegal site's frequent blackouts.

Victoria sat down at her desk again. She opened the book to a place she'd marked for her attention last time, *De corporem mentemque domination*, set her Latin-English dictionary out next to it, and set to figuring out how to turn human beings into shells for her will. The book spoke:

Velle harpazein uteri cordem, psycham, et ultime carnem. Tibi id est; in manum tuam duc voluntatem eius: humani aut vampiris, puellae aut pueri, feminae aut viri, patrician aut plebiani, voluntatum eius tibi est.

I stared at the page and spoke back, "Potestate, darling, I'm intrigued. How do I go about bending my enemy's will to mine? I have an enemy I'd like to take care of."

Victoria, love, I know what you need to take care of Captain Daylight. I can tell you what you want to know. They may be many, but Daylight is human. You have a latent power, one you have never tried to put to use. I want you to try it.

I looked down at the text, which had once again changed. It showed a diagram of a vampire and a human side by side, with labels and an explanation wrapped around. "So this is how to bend a human being to my will," Victoria muttered.

"What's going on?"

Victoria drew herself out of the book, which had become easier with time and trial, and turned to find Miles seated next to her. "Miles? I've been getting into this." Victoria gestured to the book and her various language aids. Her laptop's screen had blacked out to save power and the Latin-English dictionary and *De Innaturale Potestate* sat open on the desk.

"It's been a week: and not for the first time. The others and I are worried you've become obsessed."

"I kind of have," Victoria answered, "What this has is extraordinary. I'm reading up on techniques to control the body of an enemy, turning it into an obedient puppet, or shell for your will instead of that of its owner, whichever phrasing is more apt. I would love to see the look on Captain Daylight's face as his soldiers turn on him instead of looping around his target." A nasty giggle escaped her mouth.

"Is that what you're looking at right now?"

"Of course it is. My dear Potestate has much more to tell me about it, though." Victoria smiled.

"We're about to go check on Mara, Ara insisted, but I'm needed here. Would you be me and make sure Ara comes back without Mara. We can't take her in and I know I'd be obliged to take her in if Ara brought her back with her."

"Of course. I'll be Ara's chaperone on her visit to Mara's insanity." Miles nodded and got up. He turned back towards her at the threshold.

"Victoria,"

"Mmm?"

"If you can turn his own guns on Captain Daylight or one of his men, do it." He walked out, feet setting on the floor with a hard and regular beat. Victoria packed up her books for the road.

Chapter 3

Ara got behind the wheel while Victoria was still finishing packing the trunk. Victoria got in and asked, "Is there any reason we need to check in on Mara now?" Ara kept staring ahead at the road, so Victoria let the question go.

They had passed through the Rockies and gotten into the prairies by the time Ara answered Victoria: "I can feel as if something is about to happen to her. I don't know why. It also seems as if you should be there with her too." The low hills rolled off into the distance, and Ara stared fixedly at the road ahead. "If you were a woman of faith, I would tell you God told me to go to Mara, but you're not, so I won't bother with something I know won't work."

"I get it", *sort of*, "there is no good reason. Mara has an ongoing problem and now is as good a time as any." Victoria turned to the side window, "I like to look at the abandoned buildings; when we last passed by here, that roof was still standing."

"It was."

They eventually reached the entrance to Mara's home beneath a funeral parlor. The undertaker let us in with only a lingering glance, a rustle of fabric as he closed the door, and a muted jingle as he handed over a set of keys to get us down to Mara. We stepped down the stairs to the basement, walked past the cool rooms where the bodies were prepared to a locked door in the back corner of the building. Ara opened it and I followed, down a set of bare lumber stairs lit by a single bulb at the landing. I closed the door behind us.

Somewhere in the maze of unused service tunnels at the bottom of the stairs, Mara awaited us. "Mara," Ara called, "we've come for you, Victoria and I."

I followed her across the landing to a door with open air above it. Ara opened it and walked into a room with a bare concrete floor. Mara was sitting on it, curled inward on herself.

"Mara? We're here, can you hear me?"

Mara shuddered, the black lace on her billowy dress shaking, "The furnace used to be here. Now there's just a pile of metal and rust down here; the furnace is upstairs." Mara raised her head to look at the two. Although they had both expected to see something like this, Victoria and Ara were still surprised by what they saw. Victoria stared at the flesh of her face: it had faded grey and sagged, almost as though it had both aged and rotted since she'd last seen Mara.

"I feel I need fear the fire less each day," Mara continued to speak, "I have suffered much in this life."

"Good Lord," Ara continued, "you've gone too far with this. I'll go get you some real blood, with Victoria here, we'll get you fixed. There's no need for you to rot."

Mara shuddered to her feet, "There is a world of need. It is beyond my knowledge how much I have destroyed to feed and conceal myself. I should and shall suffer for it; better here than in the world of permanence."

As they got into the thick of a theological argument over the rights and wrongs of Mara's life, Victoria's attention drifted. She thought back to the latent ability that the book had promised she possessed. Victoria reached into her mind, feeling for the power.

Far at the back, Victoria felt something, a coiled striker hung off the inner wall of her skull. She was jarred from her reverie by Mara, who crossed the room with a swiftness to deny her debility and lay a hand on Victoria. Ara stood back where the two of them had drifted in conversation together.

Victoria startled at the sudden sight of Mara's sunken, heavy eyes. Mara spoke, "I can see what you want to do".

Mara grasped into Victoria's shoulder as Victoria stood paralyzed by bewilderment. "My free will is precious," Mara's voice came out from a thin, dry throat. "I hold the keys to this castle of flesh, not you.

KEEP TO YOURSELF." The impossible force of the last echoed in the unadorned concrete room.

I stared at her. "Mara," I said, "I have come to believe that I might be able to coerce my enemies to fight each other instead of me with my mind. I was idly fidgeting with the tool I have to do that." Victoria was caught stuck in her tracks for a moment, "out of boredom…"

"That's enough," snapped Mara, "you will do such disgusting things with this power; I don't care anymore. It's your problem. And my devotion is my business." Mara had turned back to Ara.

"I don't believe any divine power would want you to do this to yourself," Ara's loss was apparent, her voice faded despite an effort to sound normal. It showed over the length of the room.

"They have told me otherwise." Mara's face softened, "I can tell you love me, but everyone and everything I have loved has been dead for at least a hundred years. My life here is not everlasting." The flowing folds of her dress, despite their volume, could not hide the unnatural shape Mara's body had taken. It especially had no effect on the smell emanating from her as she jankily walked deeper into the basement.

Victoria sighed, really noticing the scent of rot for the first time. Mara had been rotting like a corpse for some time now; at a slower rate than would be natural for a dead body, but she was rotting nonetheless. Ara broke down into tears, rubbing at her eyes and whispering to herself; Victoria counted down the seconds before she could reasonably convince her to leave.

Victoria then took Ara by the arm and up the stairs. They got into the car. Victoria drove them to their friends' local coven. She pulled the car past the hedge of dense trees and up the driveway to a slightly neglected house with vigorous, draping creepers screening its verandah all the way around, hiding the first-floor windows and doors from view. Victoria parked in the driveway.

She got out of the car and walked around the hood of the car. A glance behind her showed that Ara had also gotten out of the car, after the delay of a lingering gaze into the distance. Ara joined Victoria as soon as she had reached the passenger side.

They walked up the stairs and past the light curtain of vines to the door. Victoria approached, and the door opened before she could knock. Standing inside was exactly who they wanted to meet.

"It's good to see you both," Theodora pulled back to let them through the door. "Come in, I have a room set up." I followed her into a dim and stale front parlor.

"How long has this furniture been here?" Theodora looked towards the question and told Victoria, "It's been here since we got this building. There's nothing wrong with it. So the room has a residual art deco style."

Ara sat down in a chair facing the room's central coffee table. "I think you know who brought me into town; I'm worried about Mara. How has she been in my absence?" Victoria settled on the sofa next to Theodora.

"She's set on living off dead blood until she can't anymore." Theodora adjusted herself in her seat and continued: "Did she describe her reasoning to you?" Seeing the blank reaction from her audience, Theodora continued, "Maria has had a long life, one that has begun to weigh on her."

"I don't claim to be an authority on either her life or her current state of mind, but when Mara was considering taking on the burden she now bears, she spoke to me. We spent a few hours together, the conversation being driven by Mara's need to make sense of herself. She started out by asking me about my religion; I responded as my custom and Mara went on to answer the same for herself through a story."

"It started with how she became a vampire, but then went into detail on how she took the name Mara."

"Maria Jaramillo was in her prime. She accepted a proposal of marriage from one of us and was turned 'to be the completion of her husband': both being vampire, they could commit to the marriage as equals. She lived for a few hundred years with her husband, Xavier Castillano, but he eventually succumbed in a carriage splinter accident."

"Upon the death of her husband, Maria wandered the Southwest. The absence of her centuries-accustomed role set her at a loss to herself. Eventually, Maria became obsessed with the book of Ruth and increasingly identified with the two main women: Naomi and the titular Ruth."

"Upon the death of her son and the loss of her status away from her kin, Naomi changes her name to Mara, showing the bitterness of her life. Naomi's daughter-in-law Ruth stays with her as a daughter and remarries a wealthy member of Naomi's tribe, giving both of them a new place in life: Naomi the mother and Ruth the wife."

"Mara took the name she uses now for the same reason as Naomi did, but our Mara did not find a blessed end to her bitterness like her namesake did. She eventually stopped her wandering, but never did find a new place for herself to thrive. Mara hewed to an idea that she had found on her wanderings: what she had become was inherently evil."

"From this belief came others, to which she adhered as firmly as a paper wasp nest to the underside of a pergola. A better analogy would be that she built a paper nest of other beliefs on the pergola of that first idea. Since Mara was something evil, she had an eternal stay in Hell before her."

"I did try to dissuade her of this notion, I tried and tried to convince Mara that she did not know the state of her own soul well enough to judge its destiny between Heaven and Hell, that insight belonged only to God. I had little success."

"Mara did concede the absoluteness of her conviction. She built another layer of belief: that she partook of vampiredom's evil as far as she accepted it as a part of her nature. Hence, she could clear herself of the evil and make herself worthy of Heaven by denying that aspect of her nature."

"About five years ago, Mara stopped feeding from live humans. She lacked the will to stop feeding entirely, thinking it suicide, so she decided to starve herself more slowly with dead blood, which in her mind is different, somehow."

"She moved into the dank basement I introduced you to about two years ago. I don't have an exact date. Soon after that, I started to speak to you about Mara's condition to help me head off her mental problems before they could expose us." Victoria noticed Theodora give her a quick glance from Ara before she turned to look across at Victoria in earnest, "Do you know how I came to be this?"

"No." I stared into Theodora's face, and watched it wear an absent expression for a moment before hardening into focus.

"It was a long time ago. I died in the famous 1812 invasion of Russia. I came back as what I am because my maker, who had been leeching off Napoleon's army, decided that I had died so nobly that he had to have me with him, if not forever, then at least long enough to find out if he liked me enough to stay together forever."

"I too had been following the invaders, I was driven by a fire of hate. I had already killed somewhere between fifty and a hundred men when I was turned."

"The point of this is, that it takes more than a successful turning to make a long life for one of us. There is a certain double standard one must adopt: for yourself it is right and fitting to kill, now that necessity is upon you, regardless of what you thought before. Doubtless your long-held beliefs will not go gently, but cling to you: cast it off onto humanity, for it will do you no good."

"You, your selves before and after, must not touch, or you will die. Not immediately: not after the first intrusive thought that perhaps something like you shouldn't exist, or that you would have feared your current self in your human days, or merely that habitual killing is wrong or that people ought not be treated like cattle."

"The drive to kill, you see, is essential for survival. Mara is not alone in allowing it to be sublimated into asceticism: the details are, however, likely unique. I was able to extract quite the twisted doctrine from her: 'I must repent what I've done; it's been so much: I accepted this fate, I exchanged my distant humanity and immortality hereafter for a long, cursed life followed by a second death.'; 'That was the worst of my evils, for it set the rest of them in motion: all the people I killed, they could have filled a city with their descendants by now had I not killed them before their times.'; and so on in similar iterations."

"Having felt rather keen to debate her for a few days at that point, I had a response ready: 'How do you know this?'; 'Do you truly believe that God would create us to be inherently evil?'"

"These questions were met by a longer version of: 'Our creation had nothing to do with God. It was a perverse conversion from our faith' I responded: 'Then what do think is the source of our powers, every scientist turned has failed to explain us as natural?'."

"We went on like this in circles, with me insisting that God is the ultimate source of creation and the devil can only corrupt creation, so our kind must have a divine origin. Mara kept insisting that vampirekind was the creation of a demon or possibly a false god. The two of us argued until the only ways to move forward were to fight over it or stop debating this: we chose the latter."

Victoria tried to read the point of this digression from Theodora's mind. What she found when she reached out was a smooth shell. She didn't seem to notice Victoria scraping along the surface, but she quit before she thought she could be found out. Victoria didn't think that Theodora would like her tests any better than Mara had. *And I don't want news of my power getting back to Cunt Daylight.* It occurred to Victoria that she didn't realize the need for some minimum of secrecy until after Mara blurted it out back there. *Mustn't let anyone credible find you and let the information leak back to the hunter.*

The conversation drew to a close after Theodora and Ara decided that they would stay a few days, and feed more secretly, before driving back to the West coast. Ara went out to the car for their stuff, and as Victoria got up to follow her Theodora moved to keep talking to her.

"So what did you do to mess with Mara?" Victoria could see on her face if not in her mind that Theodora was asking seriously. She took an infinitessimal moment to consider her answer:

"I found something that might be important, if it checks out." Victoria saw that she'd have to go into detail. Theodora had parked herself in front of the door and was having none of evasion.

"I have inherited a book, a sixteenth-century monster index. It describes a bunch of supernatural creatures with an unusual degree of accuracy. In the section on vampires, it tells of a power that some of us possess, the power to move another like a puppet. I tried it out on Mara to see if I could get her to stop rambling, but she called me out at the first stage, making mind-mind contact."

"I've heard of this power before. It must be somewhat rare, since I've only met one with it in two hundred years." Theodora cocked her head to the side and then continued, "Through this contact I discovered myself to be fairly immune to the power. I came to an understanding with this friend, one I'd like to extend to you." She straightened her head and took a step towards Victoria:

"Don't scrape around my mind."

"Of course not." *I need a better way to practice.* Theodora opened the door and stepped out to meet Ara and take her up to the room they'd share. Victoria walked out to the car for the rest of the stuff. *I need to be more secretive.* She had another realization as she lugged her stuff from the car, *how did Theodora know I'd freaked out Mara?*

Chapter 4

I sat down on the floor. My mind drifted back. I had been languishing in an unforgiveable mood for so long, it was an ever-sweeter pleasure to reminisce on my first conversion. The distance of centuries flattened the various entertainments and daily ups and downs.

I was in the fresh bloom of youth, and had begun to seek a husband. When my father entertained, I took a place of pride among the other daughters while he and his peers conversed. I excelled among them, and attracted the notice of men of my class.

Only one thread stuck out from this finely crafted image of my adolescent self, the train of events that led me to my future. One night, I was settled with a group of other unmarried girls on a sofa and we were chatting among ourselves. One of them, Sofia Mendoza, was gushing about a man who had recently arrived from Spain to claim his royal grant and prospect for silver.

I recalled what I had so often in the past; Sofia's words rang in my ears again: "There he is; I think he was talking to your father about the mine." She had shown me where to look with her fan, and I followed the gesture to the library door. My father had just left the room with a man I did not recognize, whom he was in the process of introducing to my mother.

The stranger spoke affably, he accompanied his words with the refined gestures of a nobleman. My mother led him over to my group after an appropriate interval with him and my father, who drifted into the crowd to entertain his other guests. "Don Xavier, this is my daughter Dona Maria Johanna Jaramillo, her friends Sofia …" My mother introduced us artfully, but this much is all I can recall.

I was driven to distraction by the recently arrived nobleman. He was artlessly charming in a way I can't describe, or even recall in detail. Everything he said, his every gesture was both deeply personal and appropriate to the situation in equal measure. I developed an infatuation with him that rivaled Sofia's, but I managed to project the air of a collected, respectable marriageable girl far better than her.

It was no surprise when he approached me later that year to say that my father had given his blessing to propose marriage to me, now that he had paid for the miners he had provided. It was not my first offer, but the first I accepted. "What a happy day, love," was my mother's reaction, "May you spend the rest of your life bedecked in silver."

I was giddy with excitement. The days passed me by in a haze, making preparations with my mother, listening to my father tell me what he knew about the business of my fiancé's silver mine. I was determined to do well as a married woman.

One night during the weeks of preparation, I awoke to the sound of a tap on my window. I sat up in bed, and was shocked to see my lover had climbed up into my room through my balcony. I was certain he had dishonorable intentions, but they turned out not to be the lustful ones I was expecting. He gestured for silence, and out of habit I complied.

Xavier sat on the edge of my bed and leaned over to speak to me: "I have a secret. I can't marry you until I reveal myself." Appalled, I should have cringed into the headboard, but I sat fixed in place, my eyes set on him. He leaned in to utter the secret "I am not a man. I am a cursed soul trapped in my own corpse, and to marry me you would have to undertake the same curse as myself."

I had nothing to say. I usually had something timely and appropriate to say, but in this moment I was dumbstruck. He leaned back and got off my bed, out the way he came as swiftly as thought. I was left to make what I would out of his words.

I didn't know what to think, and it was hours until I could get back to sleep. In the morning, it was almost as if the late-night visitation was nothing but a dream. My maids Maria and Concordia dressed me as usual, the elaborate finery I wore being no task for me alone to put on, and when I saw my family downstairs they were all the same as yesterday.

All of them except Xavier Castillano were the same. In him I saw a change. He had an eye out for me like he didn't usually; it had been his habit to confidently let me go through my day without the watchful gaze of less secure lovers. I was witness to more arrangements between him and my father, and over the following weeks I was involved in many preparations with my mother.

It was almost like before. I had no opportunities to speak to him alone, so I couldn't find out what Don Xavier had meant by 'cursed soul trapped in its own corpse'. By day I was with my family, by night I was watched over by my maids, who were vigilant as they usually were.

I was none the wiser until after the ceremony. We sat next to each other in places of honor; our relatives and peers came to congratulate us. I noticed that his friends and acquaintances didn't connect to his family. It was as if he'd dropped his heritage overboard on the way from Spain.

I followed him into the chamber; I was turned. Neither of us belonged among the living, after then. The darkness burned, and I piled the trappings of my former self on the flames. It closed around me tightly, a poor, benighted wanderer.

The Children of the Sun

The golden-skirted Dawn gave birth to a brilliant Sun. The Sun rose
from the Dawn's dark bed to stand as a well-formed young man. He
set his gaze to the West; there it met the First Hour, who had already
halfway passed. The hour smiled at the Sun and they joined together.
The Sun left the First Hour with his daughter. He went into the
Second Hour, who took him into her arms before sending him West
into the embrace of the Third Hour. The Second and the Third Hours
each kept a set of twins from the Sun; the Second had two sons, the
Third two daughters.

The Sun moved on to the Fourth Hour. She took him gently by the
hair, and turned him towards her. The Sun and the Fourth Hour's
union produced a son and a daughter. The Sun walked away. He
caught hold of the Fifth Hour. The Sun poured his seed into her
womb, where it mixed with hers and came forth as a set of twins in an
instant. The Sun moved on. The Sixth Hour caught sight of him, and
they fell together in lust. The Sixth Hour conceived and brought forth
from the Sun two sons and a daughter.

The Sun was at the height of his powers then, at Noon, when his
children were born of the Sixth Hour. The triplets followed the Sun
their father into the First Hour after Noon. The First Hour was silent
and distant, and the Sun turned his attention to his children. He
conceived a desire for the youngest of them. The Sun grasped his
younger son by the hair and hip. He pulled him away from his sister's
hold, away from the embrace of her and their brother. His hand
moved from his son's hair to encircle his throat, forcing them
together. The Sun was jerked out of him. He turned to face the other,
and his daughter stabbed him in the shoulder: "Fuck! Be still cruel
heart!" The Sun hit her in the face, pulled her knife from his shoulder,
and stabbed her to death. He preempted his sons' attempts on him
with the knife. He finished with the son he took, leaving the First
Hour with his children by the Sixth Hour.

In the Second Hour after Noon, the Sun met his children by the Fifth
Hour. They looked in wonder at him. The gleaming blood of the
children of the Sixth Hour shone on him. It slowly dripped off the

Sun, dropping far below to generate bright heroes with the holy Earth. His son by the Fifth Hour spoke, "Father Sun, what shimmering being's blood are you wearing? It shines with a divine brilliance."

The Sun told his son, "It bodes well that you like me like this. The blood is from my radiant beloved, who turned away from me and spurned me. Be unlike him. Come join with me and love me, my darling children." The son was shocked and appalled. He drew his weapon and lunged at the Sun. His sister fled towards the Third Hour, who waited for her with outstretched arms. The Third Hour's love was for naught. The Sun caught up to the daughter and cut her down after her brother and before she reached the Third Hour. Their blood drained down onto a forest and produced a host of tormenting demons to harry the lost from the trees.

The Sun passed into the Third Hour and saw his children by the Fourth Hour. The Third Hour, angry that her protection had been offered in vain, pulled out his strength through his wounds. The Sun saw his children run from him, and he chased them down despite his weakness. Their blood rained down onto a shoal of rocks in the sea. Cruel and alluring sirens rose from the blood. The Sun left the Third Hour for the Fourth Hour, who had seen her children die. She cut and beat him down, but he ran away from her into the Fifth Hour.

There waited for him his children by the Second and Third Hours. They stood, armed and angry, to meet the Sun. The Sun drew his sword at the challenge; one of his daughters by the Third Hour ran at him with her own blade in hand. They fought, she died. Her sister and their half-brother the son of the Second Hour attacked the Sun at once. The two inflicted many injuries on the Sun, all the more fiercely when the other son of the Second Hour joined them.

The Sun still prevailed and walked past their corpses. He left the second daughter with her scythe, the first son with his axe, and the second son with his spear. The weapons fell to the ground, where they each still lie to this day. The three children's blood covered them and hardened into encasing stone. The body of the first daughter fell to the Earth, and her blood flowed forth in a stream. At first the stream ran red with blood, but later it ran clear with water drawn up through the daughter of the Sun and the Third Hour's body. She became a singularly virtuous spring: in a later time it was named the Fountain of Youth.

The Sun, rent with seeping wounds, trudged on towards the Horizon. The Sixth Hour seethed with spite over the fate of her children and sucked out yet more strength from the Sun. She spat it out into the Sea, where it congealed into a mass of slag that sank into the deep. The Sun fell lower and lower as he weakened, dragging himself inexorably West towards the Horizon. When he was a moment from his goal, his only child by the First Hour caught him by the hair. She drew her short dagger across his throat and pulled his body back away from the Horizon. She took his place. The lady Sun embraced the golden-bodiced Dusk and sank into the arms of Queenly Night.

Chapter 6

A year before Victoria discovered the threat to herself posed by
Captain Daylight, off campus at The University of Western Ontario,
Anna Carlson set down the last of her possessions inside the room of
the suburban home she had rented for the school year. In four years'
time, she intended to have a PhD in anthropology, and the world
seemed to have nothing in particular against her ambition.

Anna set up her laptop on her bed and turned around to see that her
new landlady was standing in the doorway. "Oh, hey Mrs. Blackwell.
The cheque cleared, or is it something else?"

"I'm just coming up to see how you've settled in. How is the room?"

"Exactly how it looked online." *It was an average room from what I
found that I could afford; it wasn't as nice as the room in my parents'
house I'd left.* "I've just finished setting up my stuff and I'm about to
skype back home. If there's nothing you need, I'd like to get to it
now."

The landlady made a noncommittal sound and walked away. Anna
closed the door behind her and opened up her laptop. Anna messaged
both of her parents that she had settled in well enough, but she'd
gotten an odd impression from her landlady.

After Anna had finished with her parents, who had advised her to
keep on the behavior, she called her boyfriend. He came up on video
chat, his greeting dissolved into stuttering by their connection's lag.
"Baney," Anna called at the shuddering image, "I can't hear you, we
have to switch to text," and started typing instead.

I can't hear you, it's lagging so bad.

*I can hear you just fine, but whatever :} I'm fine with this.
How's your room?*

Meh.

*It's not as nice as the one I left back at home, but it fits how much I'm
willing to spend.*
How's it going with you?

Anna stared at the screen as he typed on the other end. She turned
around to the sound of her landlady's husband opening the door:

"Hi there". Anna looked up:

"Hi, you must be Randall; your wife just saw me in."

"And you're Anna Carlson?"

"Of course. That's what it says on the signed rental agreement I
emailed you."

"And everything on the agreement is correct?"

"Of course it is. Have you found a problem with the paperwork?"

The landlord finally came out with what he wanted: "You don't
match the name Anna Carlson. I need to know what's going on."

So it's come down to this then, Anna thought. "I am the product of a
mixed union. I got my name from my father and I look Chinese
because I am part Chinese. Do you need to see my driver's license to
be sure the name and the face match?"

Anna didn't wait for an answer and showed the card with her name
and face together on it. Mr. Blackwell left the room without a word.
Anna turned back to her computer.

Three days later, Anna Carlson sat across from the grad chair in his
office. "So that's what's up with me; I'm not sure if it's racist exactly.
They did rent me a room sight unseen and had no reason to think I
was anything other than white." *He's doing it too.* Anna considered
his initial surprise at the sight of her in her mind's eye for a moment.
*You're being paranoid again; stop obsessing and get back to what's
at hand.*

"Have you gotten anywhere on defining your thesis project since you applied to the program?"

"I have. I'm definitely going to survey members of real life vampire subculture and form an argument around that. It seems a better use of my place here than a study of the vampire in fiction."

"Ok then, there are some policies you need to be aware of for working with human subjects. There will be some forms for you, which are easy, but it also narrows down who you could have as a supervisor, which is more of a challenge."

"Of course."

"Both professors Meyers and Wilson have experience conducting the sort of subculture analyses that you're proposing, and also try Alan Birdman. He wrote a book on the connections between creature mythology and othered groups; he might be a good pick for your supervisor." He sat up in his chair. "But you don't need to find a thesis supervisor right away, let's get you started on your course work for the year."

The rest of the interview went uneventfully. Anna picked her courses and left the office. She found a place in the hallway and sat on the floor, then opened the blog she was maintaining to establish credibility with her subjects on her laptop.

Anna opened the department's faculty directory in another tab and spent the next three hours flipping between the faculty bios and composing a blog post on the phases of the moon. There was a commentator Anna wanted to get into contact with, *but not ask to obviously*, who had shown an interest in the topic. *It would do well for me if she approaches me; I don't fancy having to convince Mirabellamoon to talk to me about being a vampire.* She finally closed her laptop and got up.

Anna spent the rest of the week before classes began working on campus; she wrote blog posts as a supernatural researcher, reviewing relevant materials, commenting on news, and most lately speculating on the nature of vampirism in the abstract. That's what attracted the attention of the creatively-aliased Mirabellamoon. Anna sat at her desk in her newly assigned alcove in front of the office of the professor she would TA for this term. Anna reviewed the post she had designed to coax her target to trust her:

The Lonely Ones and Superhuman Power

I have, with much pained thought, pondered the essence of their power. I have sought out these precious pearls of wisdom, most of which I have already cast before you, my dear internet audience; I wandered far and wide, my path lit by a crackling tellurian torch, with its head as craned downward at the trail as my own. Devotedly I followed each sign and at last I reach a vision, an image, though incomplete, of the supernatural nature of the Lonely Ones. The nature stood veiled in a darkness only slightly dispelled by my torch. What I did find revealed to me I will share with you below.

By nature they are lunar, feminine, cool, and moist. By necessity they are strong against contamination of the blood, this being their principal food that is of its own right a medium for its owner's life force, hence an almost perfect transmission fluid for its owner's diseases and miasmae. Another necessity for the vampire is to hold its love for another of its kind, since their lives are so long, perhaps indefinite. Their physical strength and speed are beyond that of a mortal human, but by how much is unclear. The vampire is stronger by night, as the sun's intensity is a mild irritant to them physically and burns off the effects of their superhuman powers. On how this is the case I can only speculate that the sun, being fiery, masculine, warm and dry, cancels out vampiric powers. The exact degree of their debility by day, is, as their strength by night, obscure to me.

Over and beyond this essential nature common to all of the Lonely Ones, all of those that live long enough share a defining experience: outliving everyone and everything from their mortal life. One who had lived for a hundred years will surely have lost everyone they knew in their mortal life; one who has lived for several hundred may have outlived the society they grew up in, their country, or any number of forms of vicarious immortality. Living beyond more and more points of connection to their identities as human beings: their mortal families, the customs of their youth. Given enough time each of the Lonely Ones has the potential to become the only one of their tribe still walking the face of the Earth. This is the long tragedy of their success.

The short tragedy is, of course, their need to subsist on the blood of mortal humanity…

The post went on and on. This is the most comprehensive tract she'd written yet. Anna still wasn't completely happy with the naturalness of the florid, gothic style she affected for these posts but it drew the right reactions.

Anna got what she wanted in the comments when she checked her blog about 12 hours after she posted the bait article. Mirabellamoon had linked it to her own blog and sent Anna a private message:

Hey, This kind of information, in one way it's impressive you found it, in another, you shouldn't have made it public. There are bad people. They'll kill them. I'm a long-time admirer of your work, and though I've thought about contacting you directly, I haven't until now. This is very important. I have much to tell you. The fate of our two races depends on it. Meet me at my address: ▓▓ ▓▓▓ ▓ in apt. 307 at 6pm next Tuesday. Come alone. With all due respect, Mira.

I stared at the message for a few minutes. This was the exact level of eloquence I had come to expect of my blog's commentators, but the amount of impulsiveness about this invitation was a surprise. Anna thought out her response carefully. She stared at the message, and composed her reply:

Mira,

I would love to meet you in person. I believe strongly that we mortals and our immortal companions should enjoy each other's company on an equal footing. As the nature and methods of killing humans are accessible to the vampire from their former being, it is only right that human beings should be informed of their ascended state. I hope to find a partner worthy of my intellect and a motivating and informative conversation.

Lillianne Knight.
It was time for her first few interviews' experience to come in handy.
Anna looked up the address and apartment number and found
Mirabellamoon's real name, Cara Newbury. Anna found out how to
get there by bus and made a note. There was no need for her to get
lost like she did her first day on campus.

Anna sat alone at her manuscript with the screen of her laptop casting
an unflattering glow over her face. With the insight of retrospect, she
knew this meeting to be a recklessly impulsive move on her own part.
She recalled the trip to Cara's apartment: her last class of the day
ended at 4:30, and in between it and the meeting she decided to go get
something she'd been after for a few months. Anna got off the bus
that led to Mirabellamoon's apartment about halfway there from
campus and walked across the parking lot; Anna had been looking for
green almonds and they might be in stock in this Middle Eastern
specialty store.

There was a slight drizzle as she crossed the almost empty parking
lot, and as she got in Anna was greeted by a store occupied only by a
girl stocking shelves and a cashier in the background. "Hi," she
began, "Do you have green almonds in?"

"They're over here," the stock girl stepped down from her stepladder
and led her to the product. She returned to her task, setting boxes of
tea on their shelf. Her mind drifted back to how she got here: the trip
away from the warzone when she was too young to have a say, the
interim stay in Russia where she met the man she had committed to
be with, despite his lack of the same respect to her.

She caught a glimpse of her caked makeup that failed to conceal the
dark circles under her eyes, the thought crossed her mind that there
was a better shield against the world back in her cousin's home. As
much as she admired her cousin for keeping her veil, she couldn't
bring herself to do the same. *My love keeps going to waste.*

After she got back, Anna finally got to taste the almonds she had
sourced. After all that anticipation, they were surprisingly bitter. Her
usual check in on her laptop revealed a block of messages from her
boyfriend that had been sent during the interview:

You don't have to go through with this, Anna.

You can come home; you don't have to stay where you feel uncomfortable just to get another degree.
I don't know when you'll get this, but get back to me. I need to hear from you.

How are you getting on with your supervisor, Alan Birdman?
Are you in class right now? I don't have your schedule memorized or written down.

Annie?

The last message was time-stamped to four hours ago. Anna looked at the time display on the bottom ribbon of the laptop and did some quick math. It was still about seven on the West coast. She sent him a block of text:

Bane, Tuesday is my long day. I'm on campus all day. I just got these messages.
I'm fine. My courses are interesting, Birdman is fine.
I've come to regret telling you about my problems, you're a terrible fuss.
I'm going to bed right now. You don't need to keep messaging me.

Anna continued with the manuscript, remembering how she regretted not having just broken up with Bane before she went across the country, or right then at the sight of that string of messages. She went back to the introduction of her trip to Mirabellamoon/Cara Newbury's apartment and their conversation within.

Chapter 7

I took the bus to Cara's apartment. The building was downtown and less than a block from the police station. I had to cross both streets at an intersection to get to the building. It was a shabby-looking place on the inside, one that hadn't been updated since the mid-80s. I walked on faded carpet that at one point had been a stylish maroon, and walls with the various marks of irresponsible children and moving furniture. Its elevator was similarly dated and dingy. I rode up to the third floor and found the door to Cara Newbury's apartment.

My knock was answered promptly. I was faced by a woman in her early thirties with nondescript brown hair. Her skin was kept deliberately pale with white makeup. Her hair was slicked back neatly into a hairdo that could have been lifted from a Civil War era photo. Her dress was ankle-length, made of natural linen, a soft lavender colour, and in a similar dated style to her hairstyle. The dress, as I found out in later research, was a faithful recreation of a generic casual American dress that was popular across most of the late 1800s.

She invited me in for some tea she had already prepared in the apartment's tiny kitchen. I sat with my back to the entrance, and Mirabella, as she styled herself, poured a cup of plain orange pekoe tea for each of us before she sat down. I accepted some cream and sugar along with it and settled in to start examining her.

"Maria Cortés is the leader of my coven" was the first thing Mirabella said once she had sat down to speak with me.

"I've never heard of her." As she handed me a cup of tea, I noticed that Cara had thin, white scars on her wrists in the position that suggested an unsuccessful suicide attempt.

Mirabella didn't look surprised, "Of course you haven't heard of her. Mara does not seek to draw attention to herself." I settled in for the monologue that this type of statement tended to introduce. The rambling of a person who had based her entire will to live on the prestige of her coven leader did not come.

"What I'm curious about and, if it's not indecent to admit this, the reason for inviting you over here is to learn more about you. What have you been doing to become this much of an expert on my kind's nature?"

I've been making shit up. But I didn't say that out loud, what I did say was much more tactful and strategic: "I first came into this line of study through my younger sister." *She was really into vampire fiction, and I saw some movies with her, then got into the phenomenon.* "She became enmeshed with a vampire lover, and when she wanted to break up with him, we needed to turn his weaknesses against him to make it stick." Cara seemed to like this story. *I did well on it, then.*

"My transition to this world was no less abrupt," Cara eyed me carefully, "I was turned a long time ago, in 1867. I was struggling in the aftermath of the American Civil War, like a more cowardly Scarlett O'Hara. I met a man in black at a crossroads on my way home. I had just sold all the produce I could until the end of the season and gave him a wide berth to protect the proceeds. My effort was in vain; he did not desire my money…"

I idly wondered if this was about to get rapey; the last 'vampire' I'd interviewed, as my audience recalls, had rambled about how much he had enjoyed this kind of forceful attention from his sire.

"…Only my life. I was transformed on that day, from mortal woman to immortal monster."

"You seem to have kept your humanity well enough."

"Looks are deceiving. Even now, I cannot pass a moment without thinking of your blood. I envy your humanity, really."

From that point, I have to say for posterity, the conversation moved around in circles. I can't quote you any of it since it blended together in its similarity, and my reaction was simple, well-hid, frustration, until the conversation moved on. I can't even guarantee that parts of this later conversation hadn't infiltrated my recollection of the earlier parts; interpret at your own risk.

The conversation changed with a rather blunt statement from Cara: "My coven mistress is famous." *That's not nearly as artfully polite as everything else she's said.*

"I remember her name is Maria Cortés, are you hinting that she is related to the famous Cortés?"

"It's more than a hint. I'm so surprised you didn't pick up on it: that name, you know."

"Cortés is a Spanish name. I don't think it's rare enough to assume anyone who has it is related to the conquistador."

"But she is," Cara asserted, with excitement thrumming in her voice, "When I first met her, I just knew I was in the presence of someone remarkable," Myself, I wouldn't go that far; only if the man himself led my coven would I get this excited, "She held herself so well, like the greatness of her father's accomplishments held her up." I would have loved to expose her to any of the conquistador-haters on campus, any of them, they'd make this woman cry.

After some more gushing I've mercifully forgotten, I got to ask another question: "How does your coven work? You seem to live independently with your husband, so your coven is not a house of vampires."

"It's not like the movies. We would stand out if we lived together in odd groups like the members of my coven would make, so we're scattered in pairs and trios around the city."

"Of course. How do you feel about the need for secrecy?"

"It is a burden. I was a social butterfly in my mortal life; it pains me to be separated from myself." She sighed delicately and shifted in her chair. I began to doubt her sincerity. Maybe I had stumbled into someone's bizarre LARP circle again.

The longer the conversation went on after this point, the more insincere Cara seemed to be. When I asked questions, she gave

48

answers that belonged in a trite, cliché-filled vampire novel. She felt trapped in the shadows and secrecy, and longed to reunite with the human world publicly in the sun.

After I let her go on in this manner for a time, I got another question in: "What happens to you in the sun?"

Cara was struck silent for a moment before answering. The question genuinely surprised her. "I must have already said," a flustered look flitted unevenly across her face. Cara was either a bad actor or struggling to hide her emotions. I couldn't tell which. "I won't burn to a crisp."

"It hurts. I would burn, eventually, but it's slow."

"It was my understanding that you would merely lose access to your preternatural powers in the sun." I was finally getting somewhere; it was a wonderful feeling.

"We're not all the same. Some of us can stand proud in the bright light and be unaffected. I cannot." Cara seemed genuinely upset at the thought. Her aspect dimmed and sadness radiated from her heart to her every extremity, if you would pardon a somewhat melodramatic metaphor. Cara visibly stiffened and pushed herself out of the mood, putting on her Mirabella face, before she spoke again:

"How have I added to your research?"

"You've filled out some details," I said, keeping as much to myself as I could. No reason to scatter out answers I wanted to hear and ease attempts to trick me. "I was already aware of most of what you told me: the parts of your life and the differences in power were all that was new to me." I did my best to give the impression of candor.

The meeting wrapped up quickly after that. I took my leave the way I came. Little did I know what would follow me back from that dingy apartment in that poorly secured building. My adventure had just begun.

Chapter 8

I walked down from Mirabellamoon's apartment. It had gotten dark over the course of the interview and it took me a moment to reorient myself to the outside of the building, but I found the stop quickly enough. My steps echoed back to my ears, and I noticed another set of footsteps nearby:

Anna glanced behind her and saw someone in a hoodie with a baseball cap pulled over his face on the sidewalk moving towards her. She stopped at the bus stop and the hooded figure also hovered around the stop. To her relief, the Adelaide bus appeared up the road just then, and she got on quickly. The hoodie stayed behind.

He watched the bus drive away, and noted the route and direction, then texted Triswell that he was the one to get on the Adelaide bus a few stops down and note Lillianne's stop off the bus. Mark Newbury pushed the ridiculous hoodie back off his head. He went back up to his apartment before texting the others who had been waiting to board Lillianne Knight's bus in the other three directions. They weren't needed.

"It was an illuminating conversation," began Cara, as soon she left her room in her regular clothes, "Lillinight was very agreeable; I can't tell if that means she's a clever liar or exactly the kind of woman we'd like to join us."

"I'm about to call Kyle about our haul tonight. I just finished with the tails, unless I hear back from Tristan with her location right now…" The phone's buzz interrupted that thought. Mark looked at the text message:
She's in my old neighbourhood. Texted my mom about her renter, it's her.
He looked up and told his wife that Tristan Blackwell had found the potential. The phone buzzed again with another message:
Her real name is Anna Carlson.
"It's terribly convenient for us," Mark summarized as he handed his cell phone to Cara. She stared at it for a moment before responding:

"We'll need all our diplomacy here. We shouldn't spook our new friend with our connections."

He snorted, "Indeed". Mark stopped texting and went to the less expensive landline to call Kyle.

...I got home soon enough, ate and then sat down in front of my laptop. The Blackwells were out, as was their habit, and I was alone in the suburban home. I responded to some messages from my boyfriend and then I got ready for bed. Before I had settled in completely, the Blackwells came home.

Unusually, I was shortly greeted by a knock on my room's door. I opened it to find a vaguely familiar face on a young man I'd never met. "Hi there," was the only thing I could think to say.

"I'm Tristan Blackwell, I've come to visit my parents who are renting this room to you." His face was carefully blank and nonthreatening.

"You didn't have to come up here and talk to me," *Why are you here?*

He seemed at a loss for words at my reaction; the expression on his face shifted into the epitome of one about to blurt out a secret a moment before he spoke: "Lillianne Knight, I have some business with you."

I couldn't keep the shock completely from my face, it flashed across it for a moment before I forced it into an expressionless mask.

"Let's discuss this inside." I backed into my room and closed the door behind Tristan.

"I wasn't supposed to spook you, but I had nothing, no excuse to tell you so I could feel you out for my cause." He looked genuinely flustered. "The other Tris will be disappointed."

"Whose cause are you talking about?" *Good God, have I stumbled into a goldmine through this room? Is he also a vampire?*

"Mine. I, along with a close band of friends, hunt and kill vampires with the magical power of the sun. We're the Daylight Squad, part of the Army of Holy Light. We saw you visit the vampire Mirabella." Enthusiasm was overtaking his initial flustering. *This could get messy; I don't want to be entangled in any liabilities.*

"Who is the other Tris?" *I'm beginning to regret picking a people project; I want time to myself now.*

"She's the best woman I know," Tristan said without a hint of attraction, "We both shorten our names to Tris, so I'm sometimes Triswell, and she's sometimes Trislove, because she's Beatrice Lovell." *Is he the kind of person I study? I need sleep.*

"What does Beatrice have to do with the Daylight Squad?"

"She's the best."

"And?"

"It's a secret."

"What did you come here to tell me, then?" That question stopped his childlike giddiness in a moment. *Is it ok to write him into my project? I wonder. I must ask the Birdman.*

"I wanted to extend an invitation from our leader, our immediate one, Kyle Lovell. He follows your online presence and thinks you do good work. Kyle has a proposition for you, one that comes from an idea he and his counterpart on the West coast have been bouncing around for a few months."

"Neither of them had the platform to launch it off, so that's where you come in."

"That's where I come in to what?"

"A campaign of intimidation, that's what the idea is. You have been chosen to announce it." The uncontrolled excitement was back.

"Your leader Kyle wants to run an ad on my blog."

"More of a propaganda piece." He grinned impishly at his own statement, as if it were the cleverest thing in the world. The expression held for exactly a moment, and just before I could ask a follow-up question, it turned to one of realization. "I almost forgot. He told me to give you his email." Tristan fumbled around in his pockets and drew out a scrap of paper with the address written in sketchy blue ink on it.

"Send him a message if you choose to accept your mission." He laughed at his own joke. I looked at the address; it was unremarkable and uninformative, being made from Kyle Lovell's name on a free service. *I wonder if the professional address shows a levelheaded man or conceals an unhinged one.* I saw there was no end to Tristan's smugness over his completed task.

"Is there anything else?"

"Oh, no. That's it. Only," he punctuated the pause with an awkward grin, "I'd add that I'd really like to have you on the team. None of the single girls are as attractive as you." He ended that with what was meant to be a charming smile, but fit his stated purpose as well as the rest of what he did during this brief interview.

"I've fallen for your type before," *Sort of,* "and I'm still in a relationship with him." His exaggerated crestfallen look was almost funny. I wondered, not for the first time during this project, if I were seeing amateur acting right now or absurd emotions. I needed to write something about the performance, and talk to Alan Birdman about it. *Why is he still here?*

Tristan Blackwell did cue in that it was time to leave, and backed away, telling me that it was: "time for me to spend some time with my parents". I finally got to go to sleep.

In the morning, I went to my only class of the day. I took the email address with me to school. There thought about how I should respond in the break in my three-hour class, after which I also had to go to my tutorial session and lead it.

I went to see Alan in his office in my two-hour break before the tutorial session. I knocked on the door of his office to see if he was in, then entered at his response.

"I've had a breakthrough," I said after the pleasantries were done with, "The interview I scheduled with Cara Newbury," He nodded in acknowledgement, "it went swimmingly. I have notes." *That I wrote on the bus home.* "But the really interesting part is an unexpected consequence of the interview."

Alan Birdman adjusted his seat in his chair to show interest. "It seems our former Southern belle has a vampire hunter group attached to her. One of them kindly introduced himself and the group to me and left me with an email contact."

"I'm not sure of the group's relationship to Cara, but there is an interesting coincidence which might contaminate my project. The member of the vampire hunting group that approached me is also my landlord's son."

"I don't know how this relationship would affect my study's legitimacy. We've had a productive first few months and don't want them derailed."

"That's what I like about you," Alan spoke with a characteristic warmth, "Your ambition lights a fire in your soul. I am also uncertain. Off the cuff, I'd say that to avoid the appearance of influence you would at least need to qualify your observations by it, but that's already within the scope of your project through the bait blog."

"I'll have a chat with Professor Meyers, he's more knowledgeable about the fine points of these matters. What I think is due for a discussion is the focus of your project. You've identified a few good leads: the sexual repression angle, the historical connection and nostalgia one, and whatever you just found."

"I found more historical nostalgia: and I want to approach my material survey-style, so I can use the most of what I've found out. More to the point, do you think I should use the email address I got from Tristan Blackwell, my informant?" That question gave him pause.

"I dread this question. Saw it coming right at the start, but like the academic without a good answer I am, I avoided the question."

"It hinges on whether the substance of your contact would be admissible in the study. If you can't use it, there's no point in gathering the information. It would just sit around and be a privacy risk, and that's unethical, exposing people to pointless risks."

"However, if the ethics are acceptable for including what you get from him in your publicly available thesis paper, then this is a golden opportunity. You got it yesterday?" I nodded yes. "Give it until tomorrow, I'll have spoken to Meyers by then."

"If this is as far as we can get today, I need to finish up my plan for my section of your frosh." His pleasant smile fit the image of him as a gracefully aged hippie that I had more perfectly than anything else he'd done so far.

"Go on. I have nothing else to add. If you'd needed to stay longer, the students would have to do all the talking, and you know when you rely on them to be talkative for a lesson to succeed, they all go quiet." I left his office to my alcove outside of it to work on the intro to anthropology course students' tutorial session, and Birdman continued to write his current research article in his office.

Come Monday, I went back to Birdman's office after class. He was there again, at his computer working on an article. "You need a key to this office, I've had enough of getting out of my chair for you."

"Getting to business, I spoke to professor Meyer. He thinks that your relationship with Tristan makes him an inappropriate subject for a study destined for publication. It gives the appearance of inobjectivity."

"I suspected as much."

"You're a clever girl." Birdman idly drifted to the left in his spinny chair. "Decide what you're going to do with this information and contact me about it."

"Got it." I walked the few steps to my space thinking of what to do. I sat at my desk and checked my email. I had a message from Kyle Lovell, who was apparently done with waiting for me to contact him.

> Anna Carlson,
>
> Tristan Blackwell told me about his conversation with you. What he says about you interests us. We are going to go check if a vampire, Maria Cortés, is a threat to people, and I think your expertise will be valuable to assessing her. Send me a message back if you're interested.
>
> Best,
>
> Kyle Lovett.

How pushy, I considered the message. *I wonder what's up with them, the 'Army of Holy Light'. How serious are they?* I had no answers to these questions. I quickly banged out a standard reply, accepting the invitation to interview 'Maria Cortés'. I had found a workaround. I would include the rest of the squad and this 'vampire' in the study, leave Tristan out of it. Problem solved.

I received a return email from Kyle in the morning. It told me where and when to meet him and gave me two other contacts to the squad: Martin Lovett and Mark Newbury. They were going to meet me and let me get to know them before going out. The address for the meeting place Kyle gave was a suburban home, probably someone's parents' house.

I went there at the time and date, this Thursday at noon. I approached the house as it sat unassumingly in its lower-middle class neighborhood surrounded by other perfectly respectable starter homes. I noticed nothing extraordinary. It was adequately maintained, and I walked up to the front door.

It was answered by a man in his mid-thirties. He squinted into the light that flooded in from the noonday sun. "I'm Anna, here for the Daylight Squad meeting."

56

"Good, everyone's in back. Come in." He stepped away from the door to let me in. "I'm Martin Lovett." Martin led me down a narrow corridor to a den at the back of the house.

Two people sat on the sofa in the room: a man and a woman who were both in their mid-twenties. I could tell they were closely related. "These are Beatrice and Kyle Lovell. This is Anna Carlson." Beatrice got up off the sofa and stepped towards me, offering a hand to shake. I took it.

"It's great to see you. Congrats on getting into the Anthro program." Kyle tried and failed to suppress an expression as he heard Beatrice say that to me.

I spoke over our clasped hands: "How'd you find out about that? I didn't tell any of you about my program." That was the only response I could think of. Kyle seemed on the point of speaking, but it was Beatrice who answered me:

"Our mutual friend told us: you must know him; he's a professor in your department and our go-to academic, Rob Meyers."

"I've heard of him. Was his message about including you in my project a message from the group?"

Kyle's cringe fully broke his control behind Beatrice's back. "Professor Meyers likes to keep us out of the academic world. It would blow our cover, even though I don't know how anyone would prosecute crimes against vampires, anyway." *Easily, they are people.* "He's a cautious man." *I might have to call the cops on these loons.*

I took a seat without being asked and Beatrice sat back down across the corner of the coffee table from me. "I am the sibyl of my people, the human race. Do you know what that means?"

"Of course I don't."

"I have a gift, one that I am constantly developing. I can see where and when vampires will harm humans, and make weapons to kill them." She turned to Kyle, and he continued the speech:

"She leads us to where they are going to attack: and we stop them before they can start. The vampires cower before the light we bring into the night, the blazing fire of our humanity, the sun."

It was almost entrancing to hear them speak this way, trying their best to recruit me to join them. *They don't know their cause is already lost.* "The brightness is blinding me." My sarcasm was artful, and it brought a tinny laugh from Beatrice and a loss of tension in Kyle.

"The light is within us all, I'm just better at bringing it out." Beatrice smiled indulgently. "I have a good feeling about you," she spoke, "You seem to have taken this all in stride."

"I've had to handle worse more suddenly." *This response would come back to mock me after my first confrontation with the truth.* The interview continued with the necessities, my first impression secured and the eccentricities of my new acquaintances fading by habituation.

Martin joined us after we'd gotten into the swing of things. He didn't leave much of an impression on me at the time. I noted his name and presence for my project, and that he had reminded me of a more self-respecting version of his brother-in-law, who is the Kyle Lovell of this interview.

My impression of the three solidified as I piled into the back seat of Beatrice's Honda. Beatrice had the group set up to feed her narcissism: her brother and husband, as well as Tristan and presumably others were a constant source of praise and validation. It was a neat and simple explanation. I wish it were true.

Kyle drove us, and Martin sat up front with him. I sat in the back with Beatrice, who regaled me the whole way about the sacredness of her mission, and the glowing virtue it imbued its followers with. I was impressed with how this speech, full of vague and contradictory assertions of value, could be seductive.

Beatrice sang a loose binary: humanity was the sun, vampirekind the moon, humanity the pure: a brave, shining knight against an enemy that was both morally repulsive and preternaturally beautiful; vampire the virus, infecting its host and replicating itself, spreading until it reaches a Malthusian crisis. It took all my instinctive and cultured resistance to this sort of person to keep myself in my own head all the way downtown.

The car pulled into the parking lot behind a working funeral home. It was time for my second interview. Kyle led the group towards a side entrance that both the Lovells seemed familiar with. The door was opened by what I assume must have been a son of the family that owned the place. He had been standing at the door waiting for us. "It's in the old subbasement:" His statement was directed at me.

Kyle nodded and followed the boy into the building. We were left alone after the son unlocked the door to the relevant floor. I followed the three of them down the bare stairs into the dingy level below. It had been designed as a utility floor, but didn't show a degree of care that suggested it was still in use. My eyes were drawn to the cobwebs dangling from the ceiling, an attraction I felt necessary to resist to stop myself from missing a step blindly and falling down the stairs.

The group's footsteps echoed against the concrete floor and the smooth, featureless walls. Beatrice called out into the darkness: "Maria Cortés."

I heard the rustling of voluminous clothes echo off the smooth roof from somewhere beyond the room divisions that did not reach the ceiling. "We're by the stairs," Beatrice continued, and the rustling seemed to get closer.

I wandered over to the centre right of the room, since Martin and Kyle had drifted over to the corners. I was incredibly aware that I knew nothing of where to stand in case this turned into a fight, which was presumably why so many people came along. The doored entrance at my elbow remained closed. A figure appeared through the empty, bare-lumber archway sized for an identical door immediately ahead of Beatrice.

It was a woman stumbling in a Victorian mourning dress that appeared. She was pale and slightly emaciated, and the scent of rot wafted over from where she stood. I wondered if she were critically ill. Her hair had the dull sheen of a wig; her face and the sick smell of old vomit wafting off her dress suggested the side effects of an aggressive run of chemo.

She spoke with a faint accent I couldn't quite place: "You're shining: I can see in you the sight. I welcome you to my abode. Why have you come here?"

Beatrice was struck silent for a moment, but she found her voice before I could cut in, "We are here as emissaries of humanity; we seek to discover if you pose a threat to those of our people who lack our advantages of sight and strength." I approached her right hand at the end of that statement.

Maria Cortés seemed to take Beatrice's assertions to heart: "I am a faint reflection of my former glory, wreathed in smoke and shadow. The light to which I long to return burns my heart as I hold it close. My flesh fails, and I slowly die."

"How long have you been returned to your light?" I almost regret the phrasing, but I was caught up in the moment. Maria had a natural speaker's eloquence: the words curled naturally and artfully into a bouquet of substance I can't adequately reproduce. I couldn't help but reflect her style.

"I have found a shard of the light broken by my transformation. I hold it close and seek the others: I long to return to my creator reformed." Maria swayed on her feet. "You are here to make a record of my life?"

"I am," I responded, feeling silly about having absorbed her words. "My seer has brought me here to see you. I want to keep your life alive after it runs out."

"I am a soul seeking itself. I long to be whole and reunite with my father. This is the whole of my life and the whole of my legacy to the world." She visibly pulled herself upright before she backed out of the entranceway. I turned to Beatrice, who was staring blankly into the void where Maria Cortés had been standing.

"Let's go," I kept my voice low to keep it from echoing through the whole floor. Martin grabbed her unresponsive hand as she stared gormlessly into the archway, and was soon joined by Kyle. They began to frog-march her out of the building. I stayed behind them on the way up the stairs and stopped after I had seen them about halfway up. The stairs were way too crowded.

A sound behind me drew my attention away from wondering what came over Beatrice. I caught a glimpse of motion from the gap between the walls and the ceiling. I turned away from the three of them and walked back down the stairs and through the empty archway. Maria had taken a seat on a three-legged bar stool next to the place on the wall where I'd seen motion. She looked me straight in the eye.

Maria was backed by a clutter of random furniture, and faced the room's three exits: the one to the stairs, and two others that faced the other directions deeper into what by brief glances showed to be a maze of corridors. I couldn't stand the intensity of her eyes, so mine darted about the room; it must be an outer wall at Maria's back.

"There was so much pretense necessary, don't you think?" Maria's speech brought me back to looking at her.

"I have to agree," Now that it was just me and her. "I don't belong to them, I study them. My life is a search for the beyond in humanity. I haven't found much of it, and I don't know why I'm so moved to candor for you."

"I live a lie, you know. It seems that now was a good a time as ever to exchange confessions." Maria continued: "I am not the daughter of the famous conquistador and Malintzin. I was made from the marriage of the lady Malintzin and her husband, Juan Jaramillo."

"It's been so long since I was last human, I've found myself remembering less and less of it. The details have hazed: elements of fantasy have seeped into them. I love the mountains of my home, I love its security, the absolute safety felt by a child never touched by mortal peril. I lost it all at once: home, innocence, and humanity."

"I can almost believe you," I took the natural pause as my moment, "I can almost believe you've lived for five hundred years and can barely remember your own childhood."

I got an indulgent smile for that, and an odd comment: "Tell your friend, when you leave these, 'you'll die before you're old'. She'll know what I mean."

Before I could react Maria Jaramillo got up and walked deeper into the labyrinth. I stood stunned for a moment before turning and leaving myself. My ride might already be gone. *I don't fancy guessing which bus to take home.*

I retraced my path in, the harassed-looking son locking the door to Maria's basement behind me. He mumbled opaquely about the risk and hassle of having to feed the monster as I passed.

The others were gathered in the car, sticking out in their casual dress as the crowd for a viewing started to populate the parking lot. I took the front seat, since Kyle was in the back fussing over Beatrice this time.

Martin took the wheel on the way back to the house we met. I regaled them on Maria's mental state and likely status as a terminal cancer patient over the ride, finishing before we arrived. The two men went into the house to take care of Beatrice. I went home on the bus.

My life went as usual for a week. My long day came back around and I went to my morning class. The lecture went as well as it usually did when I didn't do the reading: I wrote down more than I would have otherwise and when I had to spoke vaguely, pulling answers and comments out of what had already been said. I left the class feeling appraised of the material, and went to spend my break in my office.

I sat with my laptop to check my email before my tutorial session. My page of reminder notes and discussion questions was folded in my laptop's protector sleeve, ready for the session at 2:30. As it loaded, my mind drifted to the Daylight Squad. I found food for my obsession in my inbox.

I clicked on the email from Kyle.

> Anna,
>
> I found you impressive. After talking it over with the rest of the squad, I decided to let you in on our primary activity, a vampire hunt. Beatrice has seen an opportunity for us to strike before people are killed. I want to know your impressions of us and our process after we're done.
>
> Meet us after school? We'll be in that one-way street beside the Social Sciences Building at 5:30. Tell me if you can't make it.
> Sincerely Yours,
> Kyle Lovell.

Quite the pushy manipulator, phrasing it like that. *It takes stronger psychological tricks than that to beat me.* Except I was playing along for the information, so of course I'd go. If I quickly left at the end of my office hour, I would be able to stash away my valuables before I leave. 2:30- 3:30 would be my tutorial session, 3:30-4:30 my office hour, and 4:30 to 5:30 my window to stash my stuff. I would need the whole hour to bus back and forth from my room.

This tutorial session was the final one of the year, and accordingly it was a review session. I opened the floor to questions about the exam after a broad discussion of a few course themes. I was rather proud of it. I managed to elegantly remind my students of all the foci of the course and point them to what to study in one discussion. The very last thing I did was hand out their graded final papers, which at least one of them had in front of their face as they filed out of the room.

No one usually came to my office hour, so I usually just did some research or writing until time ran out, or dicked around. Today was different. One of my tutorial students was struggling with living away from home and the pressure of the end of term, and after I'd answered his question about his final paper wouldn't shut up about his problems. He had shown up about ten minutes before the end of the hour and lingered talking for fifteen minutes after it was over. I did eventually shoo him away to go talk to the Student Success Centre, which may or may not be able to help, because I sure as hell didn't want to.

The delay made me miss the bus, and with it my window of opportunity to stash my bag safely away at home: schoolbooks, laptop, and wallet included. I had my tiny notebook with a pen in my pocket, and I stuck my wallet in my other pocket, but that still left my valuable laptop and books with nowhere to go. They were too cumbersome to take with me, and held all my work on my thesis project. After a seeming eternity of spinning my mental wheels passed over a few seconds, I thought of a place to stow it.

I walked to my thesis supervisor's office and unlocked the door. I hid my bag inside a battered nightstand too ugly for his home and too functional to throw out that Alan was using to set things down right as he entered the room. I lifted out the bottom drawer and set the bag down on the floor underneath, concealing it with the drawer. I was finally ready to go meet the 'Daylight Squad'.

Chapter 9

I couldn't help but question my judgement in agreeing to join these clowns on their 'vampire hunt' as I got into the minivan. The group's leader, Kyle now, sat across the middle row aisle, staring me down intently as if struggling to decipher how sincere I was. *If Captain Daylight could see what I was thinking, I'd be out right now. Ha. I'm faking this all. I'm a phony and you can't tell.*

Up front, the second-in command rode shotgun and directed one of the regular members on where to drive. The final few sat in the back. Perry Blackwell, the other of my landlord's sons, sat in the middle holding the magic blades across his and the others' laps. Just as I was getting into daydreaming about the upcoming confrontation, thinking about what I'd do with this information in my thesis paper and what I'd do if the 'vampire' wasn't in on it, Kyle Lovell spoke to me and broke my focus.

"What do you think of our operation?"

"It's far more organized than I'd expected." *That much was true.*

"It needs to be. We are at a severe disadvantage."

"Humanity can be a bummer like that." That comment drew a snort of laughter from someone, not Perry, in the back. My target was less amused. I kept talking.

"Come on, we're prepared, we're coming in strength. Is this a no jokes allowed car ride? I didn't know."

"This is your attitude after your experience." He was looking suspiciously at me.

"It would have been my attitude back then if I could have fallen back on this sort of an organization. Good cheer is a pillar of strength, isn't it?"

"It must bring up some memories," he insisted. *There goes my smugness, I was having such a good time.*

"Now that you've brought me down it does; I'm beginning to think the others' tales of your great leadership and emotional support are exaggerated." *Time for some serious pretending.*

The van pulled into a parking lot. We were at a nondescript public building. "Ok everyone", began the second up front, who I belatedly remember was Mark Newbury. "There is going to be a big party here, complete with large amounts of alcohol, loud music, and a dark venue. This event is a soft target for vampire feeding."

"We'll float soberly around the crowd during the event. When it's winding down; Tris, Perry, Martin, and myself will pretend to drunkenly stumble into the green space over there," He pointed to the green strip that followed the river on both sides through town, "and the rest of you will activate the Daylight Blades from the safety of the building's not nearly secure enough basement."

Kyle nodded in acknowledgement and approval of the plan. Norah was the first to step out of the car, *I'm doing well with their names now*, and I got out of the only back door of the minivan, letting everyone else follow me out. The car was responsibly locked, and we went inside.

The team milled about the party, blending expertly. Something I knew to expect, but hadn't occurred to any of them, happened after I had spent about half an hour attached at the hip to Norah, attempting to be her wingman as she hit on every man who was even remotely attractive. Apparently this was what Norah and her second always did in these types of operations, at least that was what she told me after the group had split up into pairs and one trio.

One of my new friend's indiscriminate targets purposely and dramatically turned from Norah to me. *This come-on.* "Hey there, I can't help noticing that you outshine your friend. It's great that you're supportive of her quest for a man, but I want you." He talked quickly to preclude interruption, but I did get a word in:

"I'll be sure to pass that on to my boyfriend," I imitated his fast-talking, "He's here today. Wanna see?" I gestured with my face towards the burliest man in the room, and the guy ran away as fast as the crowd would let him. I laughed uncontrollably; that gambit had never paid off this well for me before. Norah looked miffed.

"Why did you reject him?" Her tone was lost to the effort it took to be heard over the music. "He doesn't look half bad."

"He's short, greasy, and is wearing too much cologne. I suspect he's covering up his dick rot." I spotted him across the room, "Look, he's hitting on someone else already." Norah didn't seem to understand my thought, but she moved on.

We mingled until Norah got the signal text. Then we snuck into the basement through the hallway that also led to the bathroom to join Kyle. He set up a ring of candles around us, placing them strategically to avoid igniting the stacks of trash that were everywhere. Norah pulled a box with no obvious way to be opened from her purse and set it in the centre of the circle. She had also pulled out a page of notes.

Kyle sat next to Norah facing the box, I sat down with them the same way. Norah set her page down in front of her and offered her hands, one to each of us. We sat, forming a circle within the circle, and Norah told me what we were doing:

"The daylight blades' magic needs to be activated and powered. The box is its battery; we need to connect it to the daylight arsenal the squad out there has so they can bind and kill the vampires stalking this party. Repeat after me:"

Kyle's phone buzzed and he informed us that we were needed now. A vampire had been found lying in wait in the bushes outside. Norah called out the chant to be repeated by the two of us, Kyle and me.

This went on until the box seemed to emit delicate tendrils of faint light. They curled towards the river side of the building. That was when Norah ceased to call out the chant, and Kyle and I stopped returning it. We waited on word from outside.

Kyle's phone buzzed with another text: "They have a live capture; something weird happened and Perry wants to get to the bottom of it," was his summary of the message's contents. *So they've caught a 'vampire'. I wonder what their friend will be doing. Will it be Cara?*

We left the basement, splitting up to exit by different ways so our illicit usage of the space would be less noticeable. Norah blew out and gathered the candles, leaving last. I congratulated the star of the party for his promotion when I bumped into him on my way out. I made it back to the parking lot to find Kyle had already met up with the others.

He was packing something into the trunk as I approached. As the hatchback slammed shut, I caught a glimpse of a body in the trunk. It was dead or unconscious by the way it moved. I couldn't tell which. I waited until I got close enough to see that the body in the trunk was a young woman.

"What's going on?" I kept my tone deliberately casual. Kyle glanced over his shoulder at me; he seemed mildly surprised at my appearance. There could have been more emotion hidden under his face.

"We have the vampire Beatrice foresaw killing here. She tried something odd, a mental attack, on Mark. I'm going to take her to the family cottage for Beatrice to investigate." *Something must be showing on my face*, I thought, *they're surrounding me.* I started to babble about the authorities and what they were doing and, I'm ashamed to recall, the next thing I did as they closed around me is hyperventilate into a faint.

Chapter 10

Victoria had gone out to feed. She saw on TV that there was an event going on near the Thames, and in agreement with Ara and Theodora decided that it would provide an ideal easy feed for them. She hung out nearby, in the green area that formed flood zone along the river, waiting for drunk partiers to spill over from the venue. Ara waited about a hundred feet downriver from her.

It was almost unendurably boring at first, like these stakeouts always were. Victoria sat in the bushes and practiced looking drunk into the small mirror she'd brought for the purpose, waiting to stumble out and ambush someone impaired. The music thumped electronically inside, and finally people started to drift out of the hall at around 1 am.

At first, they walked calmly and collectedly to their cars or cabs. I sat expectantly, waiting for someone to be too drunk to drive, unwilling or unable to pay for a cab, and attempt to cut through the woods on the way home to the nearby neighborhoods.

At long last, a group of four stumbled out of the concert and towards the woods. They spent about five minutes in the parking lot struggling to string together coherent sentences about whether they should pay for a cab or stumble back to their frat, cutting the trip to about a block by going through the woods.

No one was willing to pay up, so the woods it was. They were four young men, and as I watched them come towards me, I had an idea. It was a rather obvious thought: these prey items will be my next attempt at puppeting. I reached back into my mind and found my psychic arms.

As they came closer, I made contact with the mind of the one closest to me. He was the oldest of the group, and he wore his leadership of the group with pride. It was the first thing I found when I made contact. My next discovery was better, though. They were a Daylight Squad.

I kept swiping at his mind: after I had pulled the topmost two sheets of thought from his mind, I couldn't grasp the underlying layers. My psychic arm thrashed clumsily and struggled to reveal more of the middle-aged, midlevel member of the Daylight Squad's thoughts as he pretended to drunkenly shuffle into the woods with his fellow squad members. None of them were actually drunk. All of them were surreptitiously scanning the underbrush.

The leader stopped in his tracks, suddenly confused. Another of the men noticed the change immediately: "Hey, something's off about him. Get the phone." He glanced towards another of the squad, unwilling to keep his eyes off their surroundings for long. A third man pulled a cell phone out of his pocket, presumably to call emergency services for what they must think is a medical problem.

The replacement leader looked up from holding the first man steady; his name is Mark Newbury, I read off the top mind page. The replacement, I attempted to read his mind for a name, but my arms flapped lazily and uselessly rustled the grass by the group's feet. I couldn't get them to coordinate so I retracted them; I immediately felt drained. *So that's the problem. I've been burning too much energy; it's good there's so much more of it so close.*

The replacement spotted me in the bushes and I fake drunkenly, and really exhaustedly, stumbled out of the bushes. "Wild party!" I screamed atonally at them. "I don't know who's celebrating what, but they throw a great party! Woooo!" I let out a calculatedly woozy laugh, shifting between high and low volume in waves as I wavered deliberately towards them.

I could feel them tense up. They knew what I was and did not like that they were without the support of their tactical leader. I got within striking distance. I couldn't believe my luck. I was so sure that I'd be able to kill the two I had no use for, throw one to Ara, and drain the last in no time at all. The anticipation was almost too much. I heard the buzz of a phone on vibrate, and the group's attitude changed in an instant.

They dropped all the pretense and moved normally, the two who were neither the leader nor his replacement pulling glowing blades out from the folds of their coats. The windowless wall of the venue stared blankly on the scene, mute to inform its occupants of the fight that had just started. I did the same, cracking an even, predatory smile to replace the lopsided false one I'd worn before.

I again readied my psychic arm, this time to strike bluntly and stun one of my opponents to better eliminate the others. I hit a brick wall. The replacement pulled a glowing mace out of his duffel bag. He called out in a language I didn't recognize and came at me. I lunged at his exposed gut but one of his lackeys had him covered, slashing a substantial amount of the flesh from the offending hand that somehow could not reach him properly.

The last foot of air around him felt like it was made of thick plaster mixed with molasses, a brittle, yet sticky, barrier whose texture defied common sense. That was the last thing I was aware of before the mace blow knocked out my lights.

Τό Βένθος

From the darkness, the sky glowed in the East with the purest blue.
The surface of the water rippled away from the bow, belaying the
stillness below. I saw glimmers of light shine back into my eyes. I
saw the darkness of the deep. Sheets of water caught the dawn's rosy
glow, reflecting a bolt of golden brightness over the face of the great
black sea.

I saw that image too dissolve, as if its fabric were set in acid, slowly
disintegrating. The railing passed beneath me as I slid over; I
dropped. With a hard smack of contact, I hit the water in a flaccid
bellyflop. Had I been human, the impact would have killed me.

I bobbed at the surface for a few moments, but I could feel the vast
deep beneath my feet; I could feel an attraction to the void, a pull for
me to drift down. I sucked in a lungful of water, willing myself to do
what would have killed my past self, but merely pained my new form.

The weight of the water let me sink. I drifted gracefully now that the
thrashing about was over with. I looked up at the thin veil of water
over my head, then turned down to the majestic expanse of liquid
void beneath my feet. The sun rose over the water. I could see it low
to the horizon through a shallow and wide cut through the lightest
aquatic layers as I looked forwards. It shone a muted, rippled white in
the top of my vision.

The sun rose and from the surface it must have grown stronger, but
from beneath it faded, obscured by more and more water as I drifted
down. Its color cooled, getting bluer and darker as it approached its
zenith.

I drifted downwards still, buffered by the currents, straying from
where I hit the surface. I saw a squid swim past me, puffing water
behind it as its arms propelled it across my front; it vanished past the
left extreme of my peripheral vision. The water softly stroked over
my flesh, clothing and holding me softly yet utterly. Above my head
a greater and greater depth drifted.

Layers of increasing darkness waved over my feet. The pressure bore down on me from all sides, holding me tighter than any embrace. Gazing above my head, the light dimmed to a single ray in the absolute black of the deep that surrounded me in every other direction. I was certain that from now until forever, the depth and the weight would hold me as their own: I would never feel love or pain, and I would exist forever.

The water above me almost imperceptibly became the shade of blue that could penetrate the deepest, and I was immediately overwhelmed with panic. The light was dear to me so suddenly, now that the darkness had almost completely consumed me. As if my body had extended beneath me for miles, I could feel dark and ghostly creatures of the abyss brush against the soles of my feet. I kicked violently, struggling towards the faint and distant light.

Part II
Chapter 1

Anna walked up to the enchanted bars; the notebook-paper sign lazily taped to one of them told her they were impervious to vampiric strength. On the other side, someone sat in the middle of the floor. It was a pale woman with slightly waving auburn hair, the same one Anna had seen being loaded into the trunk of the Daylight Squad's car. Anna spoke:

"Who are you?" The other snorted.

"Really, who is anyone?" She got up and turned to face Anna: "How old do you think I am?" Anna stared for a moment before deciding to go along for the ride.

"Like you're just going to College: late teens, early twenties, I can't tell which." That answer drew a snort.

"I'm forty-seven. I was turned on my way back from a party in my final year. I'm glad it shows."

"Oh," Anna wondered at what she'd found, "What did you want to do with your degree? I'm one to talk, I have a premed bachelor's degree, a master's in anthropology, and am working on a PhD in the same right now." Telling people about all those degrees never did get old. Even in this crisis.

"Don't indulge me. I'm an actual vampire; not a delusional 'real life vampire'. I was turned in 1979 and I haven't aged a day since." She got up from her spot on the floor. "Let me tell you my life story; I'm bored."

"Why not." Anna sat down on the floor and got the best look at her fellow inmate as she could from her side. *I wonder how I'll get to leave this place.* Anna forced down the doubts that she would ever leave this dungeon alive down into the floor of the cell.

74

"As I was saying, my name is Victoria Falls. It sounds like a joke name; it isn't. I had cruel and uninventive parents. I was turned in the week before I was set to graduate from the University of Virginia. I was still slightly disappointed I didn't get into my first choice of college, but I was moving on with my life."

"There was a party that I and a bunch of other soon-to-be graduates attended, and as I walked the three blocks back to my place a vampire came out of nowhere and got me. That was it. I came to in the nasty abandoned house he'd made his lair and graduation had been over for three hours; I had missed it. It still eats away at me when I'm sad and have nothing better to think about." Victoria had stopped in the middle of the room. She leaned backwards to stare intently into the ceiling.

"The vampire had been stalking me for some time, as he told me. He had acted when he saw another man make a move for me at the party, he said. I don't care to recall my maker's name. Our relationship ended the next night, when I did the thing I'd read about in *Dracula* and staked him through the heart. I took everything of value from his place before leaving for my own. Disappointment aside, I wanted to find out what I could do about graduating and moving on properly from that point."

"Pay attention here, I'm serious. At the exact moment as I was leaving the lair dragging an end table worth about 100,000 in 1979 US dollars a car drove up. In it was the one who would introduce me to my new life properly. If he weren't a married man I would tell you freely I love him; as it is the statement is tense and awkward."

"It is if you say it is."

"Glad you've joined me. As I was saying, Miles found me in the middle of loading my maker's antique end table into his car and driving off with it. He got out of his car, a terrible junker that he would get rid of a few months later, and approached me. I regret the first thing I said to him," Victoria sighed. "He had come to speak with my maker and I told him I had just been made."

Miles was so handsome; he had lightly stepped down from the driver's seat of the truck. It looked extra shitty next to his beauty. He was tall, and moved with a self-collected grace I had yet to see equaled. The sun shone, glaring off the shiny bits of the truck, a stark contrast to the loss of light into his skin. I was dumbstruck; I couldn't believe that you could exist.

"It's slightly embarrassing, but I've forgotten our exact exchange. I told him that I'd been turned, describing the effects of a cause of which I had no understanding, and he told me I wouldn't have to worry about what to do with myself in my new state, after a brief explanation of it, that is. I cringe at my initial reaction even to this day, so that's all you'll hear of it."

"I went home with him and the stuff I had taken, and proceeded to sell it off. Miles filled me in on my maker's life story and what he was doing paying him a visit. Apparently my maker was prone to sloppy feeding practices and Miles was gathering information to decide if his coven should take him out and preserve the secrecy of vampirekind."

"Miles told me my maker had only been a vampire for about twenty years and I believe him. The way he had stalked and turned me smelled of rank amateurism."

Anna stared at Victoria. She recognized something in her. The same strong need to assert her identity she'd noticed in Maria Jaramillo. "You really want to tell all, don't you?"

"Right on the nose, Dr. Freud, I live with the necessity of secrecy. Of course I love to tell all now that I can." Victoria turned to her interlocutor and looked her in the eye for the first time in this impromptu interview. "It's a good thing you went into research. Your bedside manner sucks; at least pretend to care about my feelings. The desire to bring out what is suppressed was a part of psych 101 back in my day. I'm harder to impress, doc."

"You're confusing Freud and Jung."

"Am I? You would know. But I digress, I joined Miles and his coven of vampires. We've been together since."

"It's been a few decades since 1979, what have you done since?"

"Boring stuff: survival, obsessions, distractions, and bullshit. I haven't done anything terribly newsworthy. Not until now, at least. I've done something interesting now with this absurd Captain Daylight nonsense."

"About a year ago, I found a disturbing announcement on a paranormal blogger's website. It set out a challenge to the world from the Daylight; he/she/it/they staked a claim on the authority to keep vampires in line. This is the same Daylight that has the both of us trapped here. I and my dear covenmates did what miserably little we could to save ourselves." Victoria started to pace, glancing around the edges and corners of the room, scanning for a weak point.

"We kept up with the news, we practiced fighting techniques, but what I think has been the greatest contribution that time has given towards our survival is something completely different; with us here is something I came upon quite by chance."

Victoria seemed to hesitate for a moment before saying the next thing to me, but speak she did. "I found a book: a manuscript that would have been written at the same time as the birth of a divided Christendom. It's full of secrets, one of which I tried to use to prevent my capture, that failed."

I made a mental note to gloss over all the swears she applied to Captain Daylight in whatever I publish out of this, one I won't have trouble following through on because as soon as the thought occurred to me to forget them they were forgotten.

Anna asked the obvious, having no idea of the likely response: "What did you try to do?"

"I tried to mind control Captain Daylight's minions to turn on him."

"And this book told you how."

"Yes it did. Apparently I have a particular talent, one that I need to cultivate more before I can do anything useful with it. I was so not up to using my power to turn all those goons on each other. Not yet at least."

I jumped in before Victoria could lose herself in thought again: "Are you sure you can actually control people? As in have you ever used this power successfully?"

She stared unblinkingly at me for a few seconds before answering, "No. I'd tried the first step, making contact with the target's mind, before, but I got cut off before I could look properly. I had never actually made anyone do anything when I tried to save my life with my power." She wafted off as much as she could in such a small space, before dramatically smashing her heels into the ground as she turned to face me. "I've got it."

I resisted the urge to automatically say 'got what?'. I have to say, my loyal readers, I sat there and stared at Victoria Falls, the Cascadian vampire with the geographic name, and refused to respond like a clueless tween glad to be in on the big boy joke. Victoria laughed at me.

"It's great; I can hear you in there. You think I've gone off my rocker and have no business talking down to you." She made a witch cackle. A real witch cackle straight out of a cartoon of the likes I thought I'd never hear a real woman utter in front of me. That small thing, in the moment, blew my mind. My mouth spewed obscenities like a drain connected to a backing up sewer. The sewer, in this metaphor, is your faithful reporter herself. I railed to an equally effluvescent stream of laughter. I can't say how long we were locked in like this before I turned to glowering, and her to gloating, in silence.

Eventually Victoria spoke to me again. She said, "How did you get in this mess?"

"I study vampire subculture. I came expecting the simple goths and personality problems that make up 'real vampires', but I got actual real vampires. That were really real and not living a fantasy. And I also found real vampire hunters, ones that locked me up to stop me from telling the cops on them. At first it was because I thought they were committing crimes against actual people, now I can't tell if there's nothing I can do or if it's time to call the Haig. Due to vampire genocide, y'know." I finally glanced back over to Victoria.

"You were passed out from a panic attack at first."

"I took the revelation poorly and in retrospect this reaction is even more disturbing. No one here is any kind of medical professional. They couldn't tell if I'd had a seizure in front of them and was dying."

"I promise you're only dying here if they decide to kill you. My vamp senses say you're fine."

"What a relief." *What probable bullshit.*

"I'm sure it'll take awhile for the residual skepticism in your sarcasm to wear off. It's always a shock to know this shit is real."

"Anyway, I think I've found a way out of here. I found a minion having doubts about keeping you locked up here. He had your same thought: that someone passing out from panicked hyperventilation is an emergency and should be treated as one. I can tell he disapproves of treating a human this negligently."

"Bad news for me, our weak link thinks that I should've been immediately killed. No need to remind me to get him after I use him to escape. It'll be soon. In fact, I've gotten him to come see if you're still alive. Wish me luck getting him to open a cell door." My glare was interrupted by the sound of a door opening and closing in the distance. The sound was followed by that of approaching footsteps before a voice called out from the other side of the door into my cell.

"Hey, are you ok in there?" Victoria grinned at me from across the room and made the shush gesture. "Really? You didn't look all that good when you went in; I was sent to check on you." Victoria focused diligently on something I couldn't see. I could hear the man on the other side unlock the door. "I'm coming in." He opened the door.

"Whoah." Kyle's second, Mark Newbury, stepped into the room. He stared through the bars at Victoria. I noticed the air between them ripple, as if I were watching a VHS of them that was poorly taped over footage of an octopus delicately grasping at something that was now overlaid by our new visitor.

He swayed as he walked, staring at a point behind and to the left of Victoria as his hand pulled a keyring out of his pocket. Just as abruptly, he turned back to me and started to speak. Before he could fully form a word, Victoria silenced him. She jangled the keys in one hand and smiled over the fresh corpse with a broken neck. I followed her up the stairs and out the back door. Victoria opened the unfortunate guard's car and got in. I followed her. Victoria cheerfully drove us back towards town.

Chapter 2

I stared out the window at fields of crop stubble interspersed with windbreaking hedges and woodlots. "Today was a great day," I turned to Victoria's voice, "I got to take out one of the enemy, and steal just the most choice bit of information from his brain." She smiled as if she were bragging to the passing landscape, "A great day." I stared out the window as Victoria continued to talk to herself in the same self-congratulatory tone. The fields were muddy and unmelted snowdrifts sketched lines where its cover had been deepest before the most recent thaw.

I looked back to see that Victoria was paying attention to the road instead of rambleboasting. She tucked the car through a crowding of branches onto a poorly-maintained gravel driveway. The car slowly inched forward to stay in the thin eye of the needle, bouncing over the random assortment of branches that lay strewn over the drive. Victoria stopped the car when they came to a fallen tree too thick to keep going over. She got out and turned to Anna: "There's a house about a hundred yards further down this lane. It's a safe house maintained by a local coven in case they need to leave town in a hurry. This is the back entrance. Come and see how nice the actual place and proper driveway is." She walked a few steps and turned around to see me in the same place.

"We did the right thing; God knows what inhumanity they would have visited upon us if we hadn't. Come on: we aren't even close to a clean escape." Victoria stood there staring for a moment before continuing, "Fine then. Stand by the car. It has a tracker, so I, the one with super speed, will have to move it soon. But I need to get some stuff inside that you don't know how to find. So stay there. I'll be back."

It was surreal. I stood there, with the mid-March cool halfassedly blowing into my open leather jacket. I shuffled around in the mud mixed with inadequate gravel of the driveway, absorbed in my shock. I felt an out of place breeze flash by me, which I later came to know was Victoria using her unnatural speed to reach the car. At that point I had subconsciously wandered about ten meters towards the house along the gravel. I heard the car start, and turned around to see Victoria backing it down the driveway.

I stood there for a few more minutes before deciding that it was time to go inside. The slight chill and boredom had finally gotten me to walk towards the house. I saw that it had likely been built sometime early in the twentieth century as a cottage. It was thickly surrounded by trees and central enough to its lot that the road was not visible in any direction. The cottage had one floor and was altogether the approximate size of a loft apartment, if the nearby detached garage doesn't count. The buildings were old and shabby-looking, but seemed to be in good enough shape to be structurally sound.

I circled the clearing that held the two buildings before I approached the front door of the cottage; it was unlocked, whether this was the door's habitual state or Victoria had left it for me I can't say. I entered the main room, finding a combination kitchen/living room, with a wood stove in the back right corner opposite the door. The back wall of the cottage had two doors in it: the one opposite the door, which the window I had seen on my trip around would suggest was a bathroom, and the one in the middle of the wall, which led to a bedroom.

I walked into the bathroom. Some human needs had been on the back burner for too long. While sitting on the toilet, I looked around the room. Its tessellated black and white wall tiles and psychedelic shower curtain said that the room had not been updated since the 70s. The room didn't show the effects of daily wear, which would mesh with the idea that the house had just been kept as a staging place.

The toilet paper had a thick layer of dust on it, one which made me throw out the outer layer before using it. I got up from the toilet and with the loud flush ringing in the small, reflective room I opened the medicine cabinet. It contained a variety of toothbrushes, pastes, some aspirin and some unlabeled ointments. The toothpaste and aspirin had both expired in the early 80s.

I walked out into the main room and rummaged through the empty cabinets in the front corner by the wood stove. I looked in the stove to find nothing but a thick layer of ash. I walked into the other room,

which was furnished, like the bathroom, in a dusty vintage style.
There was a double bed with the chimney from the stove run behind it
on the outside wall for heat.

The bed faced a wall of builtins and had a chest as tall and wide as
itself at its foot. There was no closet. I searched the room, finding
nothing but layers of sheets and completely normal pillows on the bed
and dust bunnies under it. I found the chest full of random moth-eaten
clothes from the late 70s. I stopped my rummaging when I found an
abandoned mouse nest.

My eyes slid over the books and trinkets visible on the shelves. I
opened one of the cabinets at the bottom of the builtin and found it
empty save for another abandoned rodent nest, this one made of
shredded magazines. I stopped opening doors before I found an actual
rat. I left the cottage out its only door and looked again at the
detached garage. It was locked up tight: the human-size door was
simply locked, and the garage door wouldn't open no matter how
hard I pulled up the handle. It showed rust along the top edge, which
may be why, or it might also be locked. I couldn't see a locking
mechanism on it, though.

I continued to wander away from the buildings along the paved front
driveway. The buildings were on a slight rise in the landscape, and I
started to circle again where it passed over a stream flooded by spring
meltwater. I followed the stream along the near bank, and turned
further right to walk along another gulley that drained meltwater into
the stream. It had less water in it the further and higher I went, and
eventually I found its origin at the top of a hill surrounded by woodlot
on all sides.

I sat down on the far side of the origin cleft under a tree. It was an
oak that held a top position on the hill and had grown old with the
advantage of uninterrupted light. I sat there for I don't know how
long. Eventually it occurred to me that I needed to go back. That
deluded Captain Daylight squad knows where I live and my only
protection, *serious protection, not optimistic hopes of my self-defense
skills now that the shock was wearing off,* was the psychically-
empowered real vampire I had just met.

Staring at the sections of oak roots that had been newly exposed by meltwater, my mind turned on my predicament. I had no reason to suspect that Victoria was a reliable help, but I don't know anyone else with any chance in a fight with the Daylight squad. I can't just go home and forget about everything because the squad knows where I rent; I can't go home home because I can't arrange a cross-country flight that I can afford and is also leaving soon enough to let me flee them. *Why do I think they won't follow me back to BC?*

I have no reason to believe they can't get me at home. I sat there and resigned myself to this. Reality is what it is and does what it does; I either could or could not affect it. *I can't now.* Anna got up from her seat after an hour and a half of ruminating on her own control and lack of the same. She came to a decision, one that took her most of her stay to reconcile herself to. Anna was joining up with Victoria against the Daylight squad. There was no other way Anna could think of to protect herself, the authorities being out of the question.

As she got up and started back along the bank to the cottage, Anna noticed something she didn't on the way there. It was the corner of a tarp poking out from the ground; it stuck out of a steep part of the bank and had recently been eroded into exposure. Anna cautiously climbed down to it, and pulled at the visible corner.

A sheet of earth shed from over the tarp as she pulled it up. It revealed a skull underneath. Anna stopped pulling at it. She stared at the skull: *I almost expect this now; I've found the original owner of this cottage.* It stared back at me, silently mocking the many questions his appearance raised in me. I lay the tarp back over his face and walked away, knowing full well that in the next thunderstorm or the one after that the skeleton was going to get washed into the stream. I left the story behind.

I came back faster than I'd wandered out, appearing in the clearing to see Victoria cheerfully milling about and throwing a set of car keys to herself. She turned from her amusement to look at me:

"Hey there! You finally decided to come along and fight for the right to live on?"

"I have."

"I've acquired a trackerless car; we're going to see my friends."

I walked behind her to the car, and already I could feel my thoughts shifting to what I could and must do to save myself. I slid into the passenger seat and asked another obvious question:

"How the hell do vampires work?"

Chapter 3

At the same time, the Daylight Squad regrouped in the common room. Mark Newbury was dead and the captain wanted answers. Cara sat on the edge of the sideboard, her face in her hands as the others crowded around the table.

"This is unacceptable!" The final word rang unnaturally in the small room. Kyle was flushed with anger, but said nothing more for a few tension-sharpened minutes. "We are the wall between humanity and their mortal enemy. We have to be better! Who knows why Mark got into the cage with them?"

No one volunteered an answer. Kyle went on shouting, rambling in increasingly incoherent non-sentences. He eventually ran out of material and his speech faded out with weaker and weaker repetitions of the same few ideas. The silence returned, cloying with blame.

It broke again with a simple comment: "What was up with Anna?" The group turned to Cara. Her hands had dropped to her sides. "Why did she end up contained with the monster and why did they escape together?"

"It was my decision," Kyle began, "She reacted… strangely to the captured vampire. It appeared that she sympathized with it. I didn't want her reporting what we were doing as a crime, as if it were human."

"She must have thought we betrayed her," all eyes turned to Norah. "She was a terrible purist. It came across clear as day, even though I only got to interact with her for the one mission. There was one ideal and one path to it and nothing else was acceptable. How did she end up fainting like that?"

The question hung in the air. Norah broke the tension to press the issue: "I could tell no one touched her; I was there. How did she drop like that?"

All Kyle had to say was "I don't know."

Chapter 4

Theodora stood in the hallway behind the front door. The light from behind her brightened a ring of flyaway hair around her head. "Victoria," Theodora started, "I see you have returned alive."

"I could have easily not; but there's great news. I've found something important about Daylight's operation, a weakness. Who else is home?"

"No one important. Who is your friend?"

"An intrepid young researcher and fake paranormal blogger, Anna Carlson, I found her in the Daylight squad's dungeon. She was willing to turn them in for hunting down and killing people."

"Come in both of you." As soon as the door was shut behind us, Theodora continued, "I would have preferred you not blurt all that out where it's easiest to listen in, but let's get somewhere more secure now that we can." She led us down a narrow hallway to a back room that had been added onto the house sometime after it had been built.

The room consisted of a section of enclosed verandah that had been extended along the back width of the house by a sunroom. Theodora sat down at the central table in the opaquely-roofed former veranda section and Victoria and I joined her.

"I am Theodora Feodorovna. This is the house I share with my close friends and fellow vampires. What induced you to use our safety precautions?"

"I'll answer," Victoria spoke. Theodora made an annoyed sound that was smoothly ignored by my rescuer. "Anna was conducting research on 'real vampires'. She came into contact with Captain Daylight and cronies and was present during the raid that resulted in my capture. Anna had proved a liability to their actions, so she was changed from observer to prisoner." Theodora looked to me and I got my turn:

"I was as yet a skeptic to the idea that vampires were real, and when I came to the conclusion that Captain Daylight and crew were actually hunting down people I wanted to get the authorities involved. It went poorly."

Theodora continued to engage with me and Victoria now remained silent, "What is the weakness you found and what exactly happened to you two?"

"I am in the middle of a research project on the real vampire subculture. I came into contact with Captain Daylight through a woman with some dissociative identity symptoms; she believed herself to be 'a more cowardly Scarlett O'Hara' kept alive since the Civil War as a vampire. I met the Daylight Squad believing them to either be under similar delusions or engaged in some sort of role-playing as vampire slayers. They knew of me because they had been 'monitoring' the 'vampire', Mirabella."

"I discovered, by witnessing their ambush attack and capture of Victoria here, that there is a reality behind the myriad games and delusions I have set my sights on. I don't know what I'm going to do about my thesis or more importantly how to survive after this."

"It seems that above this, Victoria has managed to learn how to control the bodies of other human beings. Very poorly. That's how we escaped. Victoria brought one of the guards to a place where she could kill him and use his cell keys and car to escape."

That drew some interest from Theodora; she turned to Victoria, "You actually managed to do something with that."

"I did." Victoria smiled, "My power failed me in battle." She laughed to herself, "I was finally able to push through my weakness and wrangle one of their goons under me; once we were captured and I could focus on the most vulnerable member without the others coming to his defense. It was magnificent; to see the same Mark Newbury who wanted to kill rather than capture me stand gormlessly and let me finish him off."

Theodora pushed, "what useful information did you steal from his mind?"

"I saw the two people we need to kill in order to break the Daylight Squad: Beatrice and Kyle Lovell. They're brother and sister: Kyle is the group leader, and Beatrice makes the glowing daylight swords."

"Good," Theodora cut in, "between the two of them, I'd prioritize Beatrice. The daylight sword's effectiveness will outlive any Captain Daylight. I want them put out of production."

"That being said, there's more to destroying the daylight sword than just killing Beatrice Lovell." Theodora continued, "Victoria, how are the swords being produced?"

"Beatrice has kept the details of their production to herself; none of the squad members knew them. I looked in their minds." That drew another scoff from Theodora. "All they knew is that the stars needed to be right to cast a new blade, but that could mean a number of things. They also knew the blades' magic was solar in nature, but that much is obvious."

"There probably are notes, but Beatrice is, as of five hours ago, the only one who knows the method that I had access to. So there are three conditions to Beatrice's presumed information monopoly."

"I don't know how canny a secret keeper any of them are," Theodora responded, "If I were either of the Lovells, I would not want the secret to die with Beatrice. That would incentivize killing her and make her death a crippling blow to their organization's mission. The question we should be asking now is what insurance have they set up against the risk of losing Beatrice Lovell and the secret to producing daylight blades with her."

"I have some insight here," I finally had something to add, "Beatrice is indeed the only one who makes the blades, and she is kept away from combat to protect the supply. I know they're made, at least in part, from a special metal the two Lovells' uncle found on his mineral prospect."

"I'm certain that there is also a ritual empowerment that needs to be done, and suspect that Beatrice is the only person who can perform it. I am also certain that she is the only maker for all of the daylight squads, not just this one. I can't tell how far the technology has disseminated in writing, if at all."

"Then we have a strategy," Theodora said, "We need to force a confrontation with the Daylight Squad, and force them to bring their ringer."

"I may have already instigated this confrontation," Victoria continued, "My capture rather than death was due to my power. Kyle wanted to get to the bottom of it, since my attempts to use it against them alerted them to their vulnerability."

"It didn't occur to me at the time to check if I was due to be examined by the all-important Beatrice herself, but it's likely. She may feel it's up to her to neutralize my threat."

"I can say you're right about Beatrice," I added, "She has accepted responsibility for the team's safety from supernatural powers. The Beatrice Lovell I met was extraordinarily committed and sincere; she would definitely undertake the risk."

"The only surprise from her is what form her support in battle will take. In the one engagement I was party to, Norah, Kyle, and myself were sent to a place out of sight and away from the action to perform a further ritual to 'activate the blades'."

"Norah was in charge of the ritual; she set out the materials and led the chanting. Before you can ask, the chants were in Latin; I remember none of them. I think that if anyone were told the secret of the blades' creation, it would be her."

A triumphant flash swept across Theodora's face, "Is this Norah a small blue-haired former blonde with a terrible goth fashion sense?"

"Her hair's a terrible purple now, but yes that may have been her a few months ago."

Theodora burst into laughter, "Oh Norah, Norah, you have no power but borrowed power. I saw her on the street and again in her school. When she wears a gaudy pentagram she has magic; it's gone when she takes it off. You know the piece?"

"I do remember her wearing it the day of the vampire hunt. It didn't look powerful, just like bad fashion sense." This drew another gale of laughter.

"You're right she is hideous."

"But moving on," Theodora continued, "The immediate future needs accounting for. Do they know where you live?"

"Worse than that," I answered, "Both my landlord's sons are in the squad. God knows what they're doing with my stuff now." *I'm glad I locked my laptop and schoolbag in Birdman's office now. Christ, I miss my stuff and I want to go home.*

"All that I can retrieve of what I own is my schoolbag with my laptop in it, and now that I have the presence of mind to check…" I stuck my hands into my coat pockets: my notebook was gone, but my pen, keys, and bus pass were still in my right pocket. To my relief, my left pocket still contained my wallet, which I opened. My credit card, debit card, 50$ cash, social security card, health card, insurance card, and passport were still all there. Even the 3.41 in one of every value of coin was still there. I explained to my audience:

"I don't like to leave my papers in my room. Complete trust is not appropriate for everyone."

"Then both of you will have to stay here until we can get the fight we want." Theodora spoke as if her words were fact. "Ara is on the road back to Victoria; she couldn't tell me if you lived or died in the fight, only that the distraction of your attempt to use your power drew the squad members away from her and allowed her to escape."

"She flatters me. The Daylight Squad was taking us out one by one, like it always does, and attacked me first. Of course Ara got away. Maybe they don't know what a black vampire looks like."

"The squad could know so much about vampire weaknesses and really believe they were all white," Victoria finished, ruining the attempted joke by explaining it.

"In the group, I noticed an ideology." I spoke carefully, "You see, when people use monsters to represent what they fear, they sometime come to represent all manner of hated other. Vampires have been used to represent both the upper and lower classes as parasitic, demonize the desire for receptive sex, among other things, at different times by authors with various prejudices."

"The Daylight Squad consistently associated vampires with predatory white stereotypes: they were always former plantation owners, or preferred to feed on vulnerable minorities, or you name the trite, old-fashioned, white guilt narrative, never a relevant or timely one."

"They may have jumped to the conclusion that Ara wasn't a vampire because she is black in the moment, but I wouldn't rely on the same thing happening when they have the advantage of foresight." *My insincerity has given me some advantages now that I've changed sides.*

"I didn't try to shift them on the issue, since it would contaminate my study."

"Ara will speak on my behalf on the West Coast," Theodora continued along her earlier line of thought, "Her first stop is her coven with Miles and Victoria; she suspects that at least Ira and Valentin will be willing to join me against the Daylight Squad here."

"This organized vampire hunting has to stop; on this much Miles and I are in agreement. We share a suspicion I'd like to run by Anna: how strongly do you think the squads would hold together if one of them were soundly defeated?"

"If I assume that the others are like the Daylight Squad I got to know, then I think they won't hold together at all. There were two types of people that I met, at least in regards to commitment to the cause: one that chose it as an expression of sincere values, and the other that felt committed only so far as it made them feel better about themselves to be a part of a winning team that holds an insurmountable advantage, or to please another member."

"Between the two, the Daylight Squad is populated mostly by the latter type. The only ones I'd name as the former type are Kyle and Beatrice Lovell, and maybe Norah Alghaul or Martin Lovett. Everyone else's external props can be kicked out and their dedication would fall down in an instant."

The conversation looped back around these points until it came to an end. I returned to campus and got my bag from its hiding spot in my thesis supervisor's office. It was surreal, going back to such an ordinary place after the worldview-shattering experience I'd just had. The campus was almost empty on a Saturday, and I sat alone with what remained of my possessions and wallowed in my grief before going home.

Chapter 5

The coven house was closer to campus than the room I had rented, so the trip felt extraordinarily quick. I walked from the bus stop, and passed the stone wall between the street and the yard. The ring of pine trees that surrounded the property formed a two-story hedge that shielded the entire building from view from the street.

The only break in this barrier was made for the driveway, which was offset from the house and overarched by the hedge to minimize its compromise. I crossed a wild lawn that had some of every weed that had an easy time colonizing neglected places like this. A sweet smell emanated from one of them; I had no idea which, but it blew into my nose when the wind was right just the same. It was a beautiful day to waste unappreciated in a foul mood.

I caught up with the driveway, which had made a ninety-degree turn from its offset, and passed the cars parked where they wouldn't be seen from the road. None of them were the one Victoria and I had escaped in. Reaching the door, I didn't know what to expect or what had happened in my absence. It opened to Theodora and someone I presume was Ara in the process of stepping out.

"It seems luck is with us," presumably Ara began, "You're Anna. I'm Ara Fontaine."

"I'm Anna Carlson." I accepted her offer of a handshake.

"It's been a great trip for our cause that I've returned from, we should go back in now that we don't have to look for you anymore." I trailed after Ara as she and Theodora went back into the front room of the house. There was still a still-lukewarm, half-full pot of tea on the coffee table.

I helped myself to a cup and the others returned to their seats. Ara started to fill me in on what she had done:

"I didn't end up driving across the country. I remembered that it's possible to just call, and Ira and Valentin volunteered right away.

They're coming right now. I was also able to call Kento Noragami; he's been itching to get at the Daylight Squads."

"I did physically go somewhere: I got ahold of Gaius and Tertia in Toronto. They agreed to come after I told them it was your initiative." Ara directed the last at Theodora.

"I'm sure they'll all go ahead and tell more of us: this sort of thing gets so many of our kind excited beyond all reason. I'm told there was a similar outpouring of vampire-hunting made possible by the printed word, like this one is made possible by the online word, and it drew a dreadful response from bored vampires looking for an excuse to stretch the limits of what could be secretly done against the hunters."

"The Early Modern Skirmishes ended with a new balance between human monster hunters and vampires: more personal secrecy was needed to avoid people who were aware of the broad strokes necessary to kill us. On the other hand, the outpouring of false accounts of monsters and true superstitions made us less and less real, keeping more and more people from becoming hunters."

"It'll be fun to talk to someone who remembers being able to openly feed in return for giving the tribe victory. I liked meeting Gaius; I do want to meet again without an emergency hurrying the matter and overwhelming any interest in his long life."

"What have you found to help?" Ara was talking to me now. After a moment of searching for an answer I spoke:

"I've just retrieved all of my possessions I can. Both my landlord's sons are Daylight Squad members and it's lucky I had to hide my thesis laptop and ID instead of take it home before I went out with the squad." The confusion that swept across her face told me Ara hadn't been appraised of how I'd joined this crew.

"I'm a PhD student in Anthropology. My project is a survey study of as many 'real life vampires' as I can find and interview. Over the course of my research, I found the Daylight Squad."

"I infiltrated the group to better study them, and I was thrown for a loop when I was faced with the reality: the scare quotes didn't belong on the real life vampires because they really were real."

"They turned against me when I showed that I was unwilling to be complicit in hunting people, so I left with Victoria as she escaped their capture. Victoria showed me her mind control power in the escape, so my reality is broken. It needs rebuilding, which is what I'm set to start today."

"That's as good a pause as any," Theodora took the initiative from me, "Let's break: you can go ahead and find something to eat. I have something to do with young Anna here." Ara nodded and picked up her purse from beside her chair. She straightened a flyaway curl of her natural hair back into her high bun.

I looked across the coffee table at Theodora, noticing how she looked in detail for the first time: a round, Slavic face framed by dark hair that might have been honey-blonde in her childhood. Her features were symmetrical and well-proportioned, and her eyes shone an intense, stained-glass version of ordinary brown.

"Is there a rule that only beautiful people can be turned into vampires?" I blurted out the question without properly thinking, and it drew a bark of a laugh from her:

"'No uggos' vies with 'stay secret from mortals' as the number one rule of vampiredom. We're full of ageless, softly shimmering ebony, lush flesh, and firm muscle, among a myriad of other appealing features. Someone here will be to your taste, I guarantee it." Her face fell as swiftly as it had shifted with laughter.

"This is a secret. You'll find that myself and the others are extremely lax with most faults in each other, so long as the other keeps our secret." The emphasis on secrecy was redundant. I knew I had no chance of convincing anyone this was real. I had to respond out loud:

"I suspected this was true; I also wouldn't be able to convince anyone of this reality well enough to get protection from the authorities, and you're the only gang I know, so I'm pretty stuck here. Being on your side is the best idea I have."

"Not going home?"

"And bringing the BC squad down on my parents? No."

"How about your boyfriend?"

"He's useless and I'm about to break up with him."

"Why'd you go out with him then?"

"How do you know he exists?"

"Victoria read your mind."

"I don't remember thinking about him when she was around."

"You must have, but more importantly, you're absolutely sure you want to join us?"

"Of course I am. Take me before I regret it and desert to live homeless and bum showers at the university's absurd indoor athletic centre." That seemed to satisfy Theodora:

"Let's get you a place upstairs. Take the good room over this one before my ex Valentin gets here. He took the saint's name of the day he came back when he turned and wouldn't tell me his birth name, no matter how much I bothered him about it." Theodora got up and started to show me up to the good room. "He woke up a vampire on Valentine's day."

The room she took me to was clearly already occupied. Before I could ask, Theodora answered, "It's also my room. You take the little bed over there," she pointed behind me to a random twin bed against the opposite wall to the main, queen-size one, "There aren't enough rooms for everyone to have their own."

"The bed's freaking me out; I'm pointing it that way so I can see the door and out the window. They won't be able to creep around the open door and slit my throat at night."

"Go ahead and block the open space if it helps you sleep at night. Say something mean to Valentin too, when he tries to get past you to me." She flourished her hand towards her own before going back downstairs. I settled my meagre possessions about mine, and myself inside of it.

I had barely closed my eyes when the sound of the door creaking opened them again. Victoria was lightly touching the open door like she was thinking about knocking. "What?" I couldn't think of anything better to say to her.

"I want to talk to you," Victoria started, the setting sun throwing a violet cast into her eyes, "I keep thinking there's something special about you." She stepped out of the light and her eyes regained their pure blue. "You sought a falseness and found the truth, almost as if it were attracted to you."

"I'd've liked it better if I'd been able to give the truth the bum's rush. It's dropped a carafe of pain and ruined the carpet for me to fix." I kept talking, knowing that what I'd said made no sense without the story: "I was involved in an accident a long time ago. My little sister banged her shin into the coffee table and dropped a pot of hot coffee onto me and the white rug underneath me. It was terrible trouble."

Victoria stared at me. "It was a great time in my life, in retrospect," I continued, "I had nothing to do but chill with movies and Lilly. The pitcher incident didn't change anything. I miss her and I miss home. How do you deal with this? There must be so much to send you wallowing in nostalgia."

She sat on the edge of the bed. "I could've been an activist. I had the opportunity to join some hippies and 'make a difference', but I didn't. Even though I'd been told: if I secret my flame I'd die before I'm old."

"It was a bizarre encounter. An elderly busker stopped playing her guitar and darted across the street to tell me that: 'You're chosen, pull your love to the light, face both to the sun, or die before you're old.' I never did figure out what that meant, and I'm far beyond dying young now anyway."

"The point is, I had a very average life as a human, and the same as a vampire. Whenever I think of my past, there's nowhere I want to go because it's so similar to today. My friends change, my family members die off, but my life, my day-to-day existence, stays the same. I do the same things with different people over and over again. I have the same powers, the same flaws, and things keep repeating themselves."

"I'm sure this'll occur to you once you get some more life behind you, but there really is nothing worth dying in anticipation of or wallowing in nostalgia for. It won't change you as much as you think and it wasn't as good as you remember it."

The speech hung on the air for a long moment before Victoria interrupted her echo: "I also came to tell you that you can move into the third bedroom up here. The Sempronii found their own place, which they'll share with Kento, and Valentin will stay in the basement with Ira. Ara will take the spare room on the ground floor, where Miles can join her if he comes."

I picked up my stuff and moved over to the next room over. I could hear Victoria move the extra bed in Theodora's room back to its spot before I came in. I looked around the room, seeing that it faced the back of the lot, and was about the same size as my room back home. The room had mismatched furnishings, like it had been filled with the odds and ends of several different sets.

I sat on the bed, wondering why there was a spare one in the other room. The bed in this room was bigger, so I didn't miss it. Victoria wandered back to me. "How long was I asleep?"

"It's been about eight hours since I last saw you."

"And I'm still so tired." I lay back in bed, and Victoria approached me.

"What do you want?" I instantly regretted my candor. Victoria was nonplussed.

"I like you. I want to get to know you better."

Chapter 6

Summer came and passed. The city core of the Nightside stayed among the tall hedges of Theodora's coven house. The satellite group darted members in and out from an isolated place on the outskirts of town, a property recently acquired.

In the city, the impressively thick inner hedge bore dark sloes that needed another month to fully ripen to usefulness, at least that's what Theodora told me. My new school year had begun in earnest and I was sitting in the grass and drafting my notes for this week's tutorial session. I turned my head to the sound of boots on the stairs from the glassed-in verandah room.

I saw Ira coming down the stairs. Her opening line was "You like our team name?"

"You're talking about Nightside?"

"What other name was there?"

"It wasn't the only suggestion, and yes, I do like the name. It's completely appropriate. We are the side of night."

Ira snorted, "I think it's a bit on the nose."

"What other kind of name would everyone agree on?"

Ira could only shrug in response. She walked deeper into the yard, towards Valentin, who was on the other side of the blackthorn hedge. I set my work down and lay on my back, gazing into the clouds as they puffily floated by. My thoughts began to drift as lazily as the clouds. I could have fallen asleep there.

Then it started dribbling rain, and I took my notes inside. I sat under the glass in the back room and finished my outline. I leaned back in my chair and stared into the sky, letting myself get distracted by the rivulets darting across the glass and the round impacts of raindrops. Lightning flashed, illuminating the storm-dark sky a pale lavender.

I heard the door from the anti-blood contamination room shut and turned to see who it was. Victoria wandered in, her hair clumped moistly from the shower. She idled about the room before taking a seat: "Do you ever wonder, what is the point of this all?"

Victoria must have been talking to me. "I haven't since I had a thought: what if whatever it all is, is pointless? There are so many things I can't do, and so many things I can't be, because of who and what I am. When I struggled to grasp it, I realized: if it's so far from me, from my experience, what would I ever do with it? That was the day I gave up trying to find the meaning of life."

"I think that greatness is the point." Victoria stared through the ceiling as she spoke, "I think my chance to be great passed me by." The comment sat with no explanation for what seemed like almost forever. I turned back into the depth of the storm.

We sat in silence until Victoria continued her thought: "I was young when this world was all discovered. I'd like to live long enough to fly off to another world in a shiny spaceship."

"Most of all, I want to slough off all the evils I've accumulated: those I've killed, the necessary casing of secrecy, and especially the momentum of my past here."

I looked away from the sky and towards her. Victoria still gazed upwards, eyes fixed towards somewhere far above. "You know I come from a family that owned slaves before the war?" I shook my head, entranced by the silence.

"My great-grandparents were the last. To her dying day, my grandmother would go on and on about the day, deep in her childhood, the plantation was burned. I don't know how much of what she recalled was real."

"Those stories are deep in my childhood, too. I don't know how well I can trust them. My grandma died when I was six." Victoria seemed to be staring into her past, "I don't know, how well can a child's remembrances of an old lady's oft-repeated childhood memories represent fact? There are at least two degrees' separation."

The silence crept back into the room. As we sat there, the storm went on its way and the stars of a moonless night appeared overhead. I was preparing myself to stand up and get myself something to eat and drink before going to bed, when Ira robbed me of the opportunity to break the silence.

"What the hell are you doing? You've been here for hours."

"Typical," Victoria snarked without an edge to her voice, "No quiet too meaningful for you to put an end to."

"I don't think our friend here appreciates being pressed into your nostalgic trips down memory lane. Did she tell you about the fifty flaking slaves, the nightmarish fire, or the ghastly Yankees?"

It was apparently my turn to speak again: "I didn't get any details."

"She used to repeat the same terrible stories every few months back home. Victoria really fancied our coven leader Miles, and would try to cozy up with Civil War stories. It didn't make him leave his wife for her, nope, they've actually been together since then."

"I don't know what to say to that."

"You're no fun, Anna Carlson." Ira walked out through the decontamination room, presumably leaving to feed. I sat still for a moment before getting up myself:

"I too need to feed," Victoria snorted with laughter, and stayed in place as I went into the house proper for the kitchen. When I got back to the half-glass room, Victoria had already left. I sat down with my noodles and ate.

Up in Victoria's room, the book sat on its desk. Victoria had poured through it and sieved out every choice nugget on how to control people with her mind. She returned to it tonight for another section she'd found: on remotely spying on people via astral projection, which was what Victoria was going to practice now that it had crossed her mind. *I have to make it to the future, and that means doing what it takes.*

Victoria sat down in the chair that itself sat in the corner between her room's outside wall and her closet. It was easier than Victoria had suspected to loose the bonds of flesh. All she had to do was pull herself out with her mind's arms, and there she was, standing over her own body.

It sat there, slumped over and seeming dead in the armchair. I wandered away from it.

Chapter 7

I feel this account of my adventure into the second world of vampiredom would be incomplete without a sojourn with my sometime ally and friend Victoria into the book *De Innaturale Potestate,* casually Potestate. I will tell what I can, incomplete as my impressions are by necessity. I have only what Victoria Falls chose to reveal and managed to successfully transmit to me. These impressions will form the raw material for this ride-along trip, which I grant to the reader freely.

As a physical object, the book is remarkable. It dates to the late sixteenth century, as my tests confirmed. The same tests showed that the pages were made of human skin, rather than the usual calfskin. The covers were made of leather from an unidentifiable animal, but the DNA results and my own speculation suggest that it was made of the skin of a werewolf.

The two main inks, sepia (originally red), and black, each contained a different type of blood among more mundane ingredients. The red was madder-based, and contained traces of human blood. The black was iron-based, and contained what I conjecture to be vampire blood. Attempts to discern anything specific or more definite about the individuals comprising the book through their DNA were frustrated by cross-contamination, the necessary breaks in knowledge, along with the obvious degradation due to age.

Victoria interacted with the book in extended sessions, in which she was completely absorbed in it. From the outside, she would sit, stock-still and staring into the book. Unlike what one would expect of someone reading a book intently, Victoria wouldn't read through page by page at a relatively consistent rate, but she would stare intently at one page for hours at a time and then suddenly switch to another page. These place changes didn't follow any pattern I could discern.

My friend also made it plain to me that when she interacted with Potestate they formed a mental link, one which needed to be quite forcefully severed. Victoria informed me that the book communicated with her in two ways: it made the open page's text change, and appeared in the form of a disembodied spirit and spoke to her directly.

The one session Victoria described to me in detail is the one in which she discovered the power to 'puppet' bodies. It was in the summer of 2004, she didn't have a precise date. It was, however, after she had become frustrated with the generic information actually written in Potestate about vampires and magically empowered weapons and before she came to discover the headquarters of the Daylight Squad in London, Ontario.

Victoria settled down into Potestate. The book spoke to her by rearranging the text of the page Victoria randomly opened it to. It spelled out what it said, Victoria spoke to it out loud. Potestate told Victoria that she possessed a rare power, a potential that she should develop if she wanted to survive the mechanizations of the Daylight Squad. The book then produced a page of illustrated text which Victoria had to reproduce from memory because subsequent investigation found the page to not be a part of the bookish body of Potestate.

This excerpt, printed in the appendix as Figure 3, was dense enough to fill a 14 by 10-inch page with no part unused in its original form. Victoria was unable to recall substantial portions of the material. The parts she remembered having forgotten are: a section on lineages linked to the power both to puppet and to 'hold the self-object with will', which presumably means resist being puppeted, and a diagram linking the power to different regions of the brain.

Victoria took her time with this page, evidenced by how much she'd managed to memorize. Eventually, she had taken in as much of it as she could, and began to converse with Potestate. Victoria asked the book how it could tell she had the 'talent for puppeteering'. It told her that it could see the potential in her mind when it made contact.

The book went on to tell her that if Victoria were to exercise this power, she would gain the ability to turn her enemies against each other. Understandably, the looming threat of the Daylight Squad made the promise of this information extremely appealing to her.

Victoria was interrupted before she could seek the secret to performing the 'projection of the will' well. Victoria then went on a social call to another vampire coven, where she would, through no initiative of her own, meet the Squad. The road to Victoria Falls' destiny begins here

The Lady of Shalott

> Sacies que iou me tieng a [conclus &a] vencu de
> ceste chose que entre nos. ij a este dite, si men acort
> a vous. Car cil qui vostre amor a est li mieudres
> cheualiers del monde. Ne iou ne sai dame ne
> damoiselle par ensi quil la volsist amer par amors
> quele ne me laissast & lui presist.

> You may know that I hold myself in the end
> defeated in this matter between us. This I have said,
> if it agrees with you. For he who has your love is the
> best knight in the world.

"What are you doing?" Anna had wandered into the room. I raised my head from my screen.

"I'm making sense of this string of negatives."

"What are you translating?" Anna looked over my shoulder at my document.

"The story of the Lady of Shalott, an excerpt from the 12ᵗʰ Century prose Vulgate." She looked up at more of what I had finished. "My psychic arms are tired again and I got bored."

"It's Arthurian?"

"It's the source of *Le Morte d'Arthur*, the Mallory version. You've heard of it." I swiveled around in my chair to face her.

"I have. I haven't read it though." Anna was still preoccupied with my screen as she spoke. She reached over my shoulder and scrolled up. "I want to now," Anna stopped leaning around me, "but I can't. I have a thesis project to finish."

"I've got my first ideas about how to cut out the real stuff from my project, but I can't focus on it anymore. I'm going nuts." She began to draw tendrils of her hair between her teeth. She stopped to speak: "Is there any reason we can't wander off somewhere? I need to do something else before I go crazy."

I looked over the various signs of my roommate's distress: the hair that had clearly been abused like that all day, the terrible sweat pants and t-shirt, and the bags under her eyes. Anna really did look like she was about to burst. "Wanna see me feed?" That stopped the tremor of her nervous tics.

I could see all over Anna's face that this was against her better judgement, but what she said was "Sure."

"That's great, come with me to see the truth you'll have to hide." I saved my document before I shut down my laptop. "After all," I continued, "There should be something for you in return for the clean project you lost."

Anna continued to seem on the point of flaking, but she persisted in following me as I led down the stairs and out to the car. I got in the driver's seat and she got in the passenger side. A whole minute passed in silence as I tried to think of where to go hunt.

"So?" Anna had lost the indecisive look.

"I wasn't planning on hunting today and I don't know where to go."

"Just go to campus and pick off some rando." I burst into laughter.

"Suddenly so bloodthirsty, longing to see one of your peers die."

"Cut it out. This was your idea, follow through and let me see this!" I continued sniggering and Anna kept talking, pulling on her reserve of academic detachment, "I have found a reality beyond anything I would have remotely considered possible. I will regret it for the rest of my life if I don't see all it has to offer. If you're stuck for a place, just drive randomly around town. There has to be someone killable somewhere." It wasn't enough to cover the frantic stress that crept back into her voice.

I couldn't help but be distracted by her face. She got the best features of both her races: the lush, defined lips, silky jet hair and even-toned skin from her mother's; the pallor, height, delicate cheekbones, and the deep, round eyes of her father's. "So?" I was brought back to the present by her voice.

"I like your idea. Let's go to campus and lure away some stupid freshman like the sexy ladies we are." Anna stared at me, dumbstruck.

"Did you not hear what I just said?"

"I was distracted by how sexy we are."

"You're worse than the most sexist Neanderthal I ever had the displeasure of having as a student. I don't want this linked back to me."

"Then we won't go to your campus. Let's go stalk the Fanshawe College students leaving night class in, like, half an hour. It won't be that long of a wait, since that's about the length of the drive there." Comprehension flickered across Anna's face:

"Let's do it." I pulled the car out of the driveway. The intensity didn't leave her as we went on our way to campus. The roadside passed swiftly, bright waste plants and suburban homes taking turns appearing by my side.

Victoria cut into my window view in the parking lot. I started. It really was time to get up and out of the car. She smiled as I pulled myself out of the car, eyes darting about the lot. "We're right on time," I glanced after Victoria's eyes, seeing a steady stream of students fanning out through the cars. A large class must have just been dismissed.

"I have an idea," Victoria kept talking, "let's go over to that divider with those plants. Pretend to look for something." I drifted after her as she walked over to the mulch-covered bit of garden that capped off the row of parking. The car beeped as Victoria locked it behind us.

The endcap she led us towards was across from a face of blank brick. We were somewhat isolated from the exit that the students flowed out from, as far as anywhere in a flat parking lot exposed to a major road and busy building can be considered isolated. I squatted down and inspected the wood-chippered pine that covered the ground and failed to completely suppress the weeds.

Victoria loudly announced that she would go over this side of the bumper for my earring. I heard the tramp of feet behind me and turned around. A group of three were awkwardly approaching us. They exchanged glances among themselves: one of them kept going towards us and the rest turned into the parking lot.

"Hi," Victoria called out, "My friend's lost her earring. It's somewhere hereabouts." A southern accent I hadn't noticed before had surfaced in her speech. The student nodded in comprehension, then backed away and rejoined his friends.

Victoria squatted down next to me, "It happens sometimes," she spoke like she usually did, "they can feel me as a threat." Victoria got up and set off away from the spot. I automatically followed her. We kept going until we were out of sight of both the road and the parking lot. Windows glared, perhaps blindly, from the building behind us.

We found another group idling in a clump here. Victoria led us past them and into a more secluded area behind some trees. There was a student standing there alone. She must have superhuman senses to find this one dude hidden here. I hadn't seen or heard anything.

He had been on his cell phone, and looked surprised to find himself interrupted. Victoria cut him off before he could ask us what we were doing here. She had him immobilized and was feeding from his neck by the time I could register the motion. The stranger made wet gagging sounds until he couldn't.

Victoria dropped the corpse. "There are sneakier ways of doing this, of course. They're secret, though. I can't show you them and they're difficult in a new town." Victoria paced around the body, head cocked to the outer side of the spiral, staring at the corpse as she did.

I couldn't think well enough to react with anything other than a silent stare. She had crushed the man's windpipe faster than I could see, and had taken his blood with a human-seeming bite. It looked almost normal, the dead guy, if anyone ever could consider the effects of this type of violence normal. Victoria had gone on about the reassurance of inherent superiority while I was zoned out staring at the corpse.

Victoria had picked a spot on the other side of the body, and belatedly noticed my lack of attention. "What do you think?"

"I think magic is our only defense against you." *I don't know where I got that response from; I had to say something.*

"Magic makes you more like us. I sometimes wonder if that were how we came to be, the end result of some nameless mortal's quest to become immortal."

"I wonder who it was, and if they got what they wanted, how and why they started on their quest. It's been an obsession of mine, on and off, for my entire immortal life. I love to speculate about it."

"How were we created? For we clearly break the rules of life. Human blood drunk every few months is not nutritious enough to feed a normal human, never mind the various superhuman powers we possess. I want to look into this with science, but that would break our secrecy. The risk of setting up experiments… I would be stopped by my kind before I'd even finished ordering the equipment."

"Being a vampire is like being in a gang. One whose only law is to never reveal their existence. That is the only rule that our kind will ever enforce against each other, even if we follow humanity out into space before the Earth dies, even if the sun explodes or the world is annihilated in nuclear fire. A vampire will only die if it reveals vampirekind to humanity at large or there is a Malthusian crisis."

"We would, of course, need to be fewer if nuclear war or something else decimates the human population. Are you thinking about buying property in Florida?"

I shake my head. *Why does she think I have anything to invest anywhere?* The numbness is frustrating me.

"Don't bother; it'll be underwater in your lifetime. Also, too many hurricanes."

"I am in no position to buy property, Viki." For that I got a quick expulsion of uneven breath that must have been suppressed laughter. "I've done nothing but invest in my schooling for my entire adult life; it's too expensive."

"We're on the same side on climate change, great. Let's go back home and doodle over a map about it. I'll live to see it all, so I've been keeping track of where to get the best of the changes."

"I've come to believe that there will be an uninhabitably hot belt around the equator and newly habitable land up by the poles. Also there will be a fog of war opportunity for us to get established while humanity moves. Come on, let's skip this party."

Victoria led me out from the sheltered spot on a now-deserted path, talking about climate change the entire way. We were seen walking and heard intellectualizing by a few individuals and one more clump of people on the street side of the building. I slid back into the passenger seat next to Victoria and we went back to the Nightside coven house.

I couldn't make sense of my experience. I spent hours trying find my emotions to start to work through them, but I ended up just wasting hours grasping for names and getting pulled away by my need to work on both my thesis and my teaching. I had not the luxury of idleness.

Insight came to me in dribbles. As I picked up my bag to leave for my tutorial session, it occurred to me that I understood reality through evidence. I needed to see that vampires were indeed real. My lingering disbelief still stalked my trail. I had three more epiphanies like this over the year: I'm a terrible literalist, nothing is real until I could see it, no connection was true until it was seen.

A year went by like this, reaction bubbling to the surface in spurts. I couldn't help but wonder why the Nightside had bothered with me like this. I lived with them, and they asked for nothing in return. It occurred to me later that they gained a facade of legitimacy with me here, going about my human routine for all to see. It made the whole seem less suspicious, and since I was both in on and committed to keeping the secret, I was a safe diversion and a toy to amuse them.

I speculated on this alone, not wanting to trigger the thought that I might be better eaten. Victoria continued to show an interest in me, wandering in to chat about the far past and the far future whenever she got bored. One day I noticed a pickup truck parked outside the neighbor across the street's house. I noticed it again a few more days when I went out for food and for class. After a few weeks of this, I didn't see it again. I started writing a book in my blogger persona. I couldn't just let this experience fade forgotten into the void.

I finally sent Bane a message: *No, I don't want to go back to your coast. I don't want to see you again. Stop messaging me.* I have no use for someone as weak as you, I thought but I didn't write. Nothing could have been enough of a bribe to send me back with this unresolved. I had accepted the challenge, and wouldn't have it follow me home. I lived on, the solution irrevocably approaching. *I may yet lay a corpse between this danger and my love.*

Victoria wandered over to Anna as she sat in front of her laptop. Looking over her shoulder, it was apparent that Luke wasn't taking long-distance rejection well. "A better man would recognize that no lady or damsel who was wanted by your love would leave it for him." My remark drew her attention from her screen to my face. Anna's was still twisted with a strange mix of disgust and grief. I kept talking:

"Adventure has chosen you to be his paramour. You have followed him into the perilous wood, and seek the goal with death as your forfeit."

"Now you've discovered the meaning of life." A deep-dug cynicism spluttered through her lips. The disgust further twisted her face, distorting her beautiful features. "Look at this," she turned her laptop so I could see the screen.

It was a fullscreen page full of pleading for attention from Bane. I skimmed the messages that Anna had stopped answering a week ago. "That's pathetic, you'd just met in your gap year and then you moved across the country and stayed there for two and a half years. How much of a commitment can he expect at this point?"

"He always did like me more; the novelty of him wore off quickly." Anna closed Skype and then her laptop. "I'd like to have a lover I can look across at on the same level." She kept me in her eye as she said that. *A girl could hope*.

I took a seat next to her on the edge of the bed. "You never have to fear looking down on me."

Her face had settled into blank lines.

Chapter 9

Anna sat across the table from Ara Fontaine in the early afternoon. Ara had just finished with a novel and was gazing absently into the distance. Out back, someone was practicing polefighting, and the sound of their staffs thunking together penetrated the glass walls. My finished lunch sat in front of me. I asked her something I'd been meaning to for awhile:

"How did you become a vampire?"

"I was turned in 1864. My mistress and her husband were in the middle of arranging their flight from the soon-to-be-defeated Confederacy. I was still with our, my and my future husband's, master; Claudine Fontaine had gone ahead to Brazil."

"She had turned her husband, Marshall, fifty years before the war to better blend in socially."

"My husband Miles had been offered to work for the Confederate army years ago. No one asked our mistress. She just volunteered him."

"I didn't know at the time, but Miles had already absconded and joined the Union. He had been on the winning side for more than two years when my master was completing the arrangements to flee with myself in tow."

"I had no intention of going. I knew the master was something more than human from the older slaves' tell of his agelessness, and had witnessed him feeding on an unfortunate Confederate deserter when I ought not have been watching him. I put the pieces together like this: my master and mistress were in league with the devil."

"Some of the others thought the two of them to be proper demons or possessed by the same. Of the latter, all believed that each had welcomed the demon's consumption of their heart."

"Now that our master was alone and the Union army fast approaching, the five of us left with him decided to assassinate him and walk over to freedom. The plantation had direct access to the Gulf Coast, whither dear marse Marshall planned to flee; two days' drive to the East was New Orleans, we would surely meet someone. Those were our thoughts."

"It was no simple matter for the five of us to keep this secret from marse, meeting in the stable with Jim and Tom. They had little work since the horses were so few by then, the two of them. With myself, the other housemaid Nelly, and Marshall's trusted body servant Cassius, they plotted our escape."

"You can tell Cassius and I are the youngest of the lot, since the master went on a naming theme. There used to be more of us named like that, who had sooner left the plantation."

"It was a simple plan for the assassination; there was little we could arrange in secret. Marshall was treated to an ambush one night at dinner: he killed us all with the inhuman strength that none of us had known he had."

"I must have been exposed to a critical amount of his blood in the struggle, for three days later I awoke to the remains of my closest confidants, the last four of Claudine Fontaine's niggers left in the Confederate States of America."

"I fed off the plantation's nearest neighbor, and lived on. The Yankees took over the neighbourhood, if the string of distant plantations along the coast could be called such, only a day later."

As Ara gathered her thoughts, I couldn't help but wonder how much of what she'd told me was true. The vagueness of detail and shifts in tone made me suspicious, but… *I can't think of any reason to believe her other than there being no good alternative.* I don't know if there was anything extant that could confirm or deny this story. *Where and when is this supposed to happen? Does this even fit any moment in the Civil War?*

I remember the city of New Orleans fell relatively early, but for the life of me I had no idea how far out the Union presence extended or when they were where. My mental scrounging was quickly interrupted:

"Obviously, marse was gone when I awoke. I went in search of Miles. All the vagaries of finding him, the false turns and dead ends I'll not summarize for you here. Suffice to say, I heard that he had joined the cause of freedom, and I found him out West."

"I turned him, and he turned Richard Weiss. It was in gratitude, he told me, for what I never could understand, no matter how many times Miles tried to explain it."

I sat there, the sound of martial arts practice drifting over to my ears, utterly paralyzed. I knew I ought to ask her something to suss out if she were lying, something to point me to something verifiable, but I couldn't bring myself to do it. Ara Fontaine pulled herself out of her thoughts and went out to join the practice. I sat there.

The Seduction of Victory

The weeks went on in a daze, Anna constantly vacillating over what
to include in her thesis project and what to keep secret. I was of
limited help, but I did bounce ideas back to her and improve her
judgement. After I'd done as much as I could, I left Anna in the back
room with her laptop to get into Potestate in my room.

When I got there, I found Potestate unresponsive. I could only find
the information that was always there, which I had already read, and
couldn't contact the book's soul for more. I'll try again soon enough;
there was no point going nuts over it. I set it down and walked over to
the bed. I lay down for a nap in the meantime, feet pointed at the desk
with my dear grimoire on it.

I drifted off in no time. I was still in bed, but the room outside was
out-of-focus and indistinct. I felt heavy in my body, and rooted to my
sleep position. Out of the shadows in the left corner between the desk
and the outside wall, a figure coalesced. It stepped forward to stand in
between the book and the foot of the bed.

It was a huge relief when I noticed that it was only a child. It shyly
fidgeted on the spot before it managed to run up the gumption to say
anything: "You're the best," it blurted out, "No one can control
people like they were his own limbs like you. My brother thinks
that's bad but he isn't here so he can't make me stop being nice to
you for using it."

"Sweetie, what are you doing here?" My voice seemed to emanate
from between my eyes; my mouth remained shut and my voice box
did not vibrate, "A little boy like you shouldn't be out alone," *How do
I know it's a boy? The child doesn't look particularly masculine.* "Go
home, go back to your parents, or your brother, you shouldn't be
lurking in a stranger's house"

"But you're not a stranger, we spend so much time together, why
can't you recognize me?"

"Little boy, I can't take care of you."

The apparition screamed at me, and lunged at my exposed feet. It flew through the foot of the bed as if it were made of cloud. The feeling of paralysis faded from my body, and I turned over onto my side. I could have seen the glassless roof of the verandah out the window if I had stood up, but as it was I could only see the trees that surrounded Theodora's coven house's lot. I heard soft footsteps and a creak of the bed behind me, which were followed by a hand on my hip.

I turned over to see a translucent woman, dimly glowing as if lit from the inside by a sea of lightly drifting algae. Her glow was colored to match each part of her body: the waves of dim red in her almost-black hair, the shaded folds of her skin, and the liquid amber of her eyes. She glowed everywhere: a delicate, cool peach over her skin. She lounged over the covers next to me, weightlessly set above the yielding mattress.

The apparition smiled at my surprise. I noticed the sound of the shower going nearby, but I forced my attention back onto her. We faced each other, each lying on her side, propped up on an elbow: me on my right, she on her left. "I can see the longing in your soul," the other traced a line from my collarbone to the cleft of the first button done up on my shirt.

I could feel myself respond without speaking: "I can see something close to what I want. My heart belongs to another, and I'm not nearly as much of a narcissist as you seem to think." The apparition smiled, and her lips shifted into a lush, defined set in muted mulberry.

"I can tell you have a dull lump of slag on your mind, a soul heavied by sorrow; I am a luminous being."

I returned her smile, the oddness of her appearance was fading. "Indeed, you glow incandescent." I raised my free hand and ran it over her exposed side. It felt almost human, warm and smooth, but flawless.

The flesh had as perfect a surface as blown glass and as pliant as silk. Her eyes flashed white, her smile splitting into a two-halved gash. I shifted over towards her, holding a hand behind her head and pulling into a kiss.

Down on the first floor, Anna stared at the draft of her thesis. In the background, there was a window open to her email, with a message to Prof. Birdman waiting for an attached copy. It had been waiting there for an hour and a half. She stared at her section on Cara Newbury.

Anna was in agreement with Victoria that Maria Cortés didn't belong in the project. Yet Cara might, but not definitely, be a link to the Daylight Squad, the thing to which both of them needed their connection to be secret. "I'm getting nowhere," Anna mumbled to the laptop.

Anna shut it and made herself a mug of tea to angst over. *Academic integrity be damned. I can't leak information that leads to all the crimes connected to the Daylight Squad, not knowing what has already reached the police.* In the end, I worked up the nerve to just delete Cara's section. I let out a sigh and then attached the newly saved document to my email. It went off without a hitch and I was left to do something else.

I rattled around the house looking for something to do. I went to my room and rifled through the books I had left, but I couldn't settle down to read. I opened the fridge, scanned it, and closed it when none of the food appealed to me. I wandered over to the house's corner of bookshelves, but couldn't focus there any more than in my room.

I ended up back on my laptop, walking a circuit between checking my email, searching for news reports of suspicious deaths and disappearances, and random YouTube videos. Finally, I had had enough; I had just finished with a story about a high school student that had gone missing a week ago. I watched a fail compilation to drag my mood out of the gutter before trying to go to bed. Hours had gone by as I anxiously paced the internet.

The first thing I did upstairs was set up my laptop to rest in its spot in my room; then I took a shower and went back. I passed Victoria's room twice on the way between mine and the bathroom. The door was closed with silence behind it both times. I got into bed myself, willfully ignoring my supervisor's pending notes, and more of Bane's pathetic mooning messages that were likely waiting for me on Skype, and the looming threats posed by the Daylight Squad.

I must be dreaming now. I hadn't seen the girl I was walking with since my last day of exams as a high school student. Her name was Jennie or Jenna, one of those might be short for Jennifer. I don't think I ever learned her last name and definitely can't recall it now. We were just outside of my old high school, and walked away from the main doors towards a deeply forested area that was, in reality, about a fifteen-minute drive outside of town.

We walked at a conversational pace and idly chatted, somehow staying in the paved area near the athletic field and not getting any closer to the woods. After an indefinite length of time in this state, someone I didn't recognize walked up from behind us and approached me. He was dressed like Mercutio in a production that used costumes which properly belonged in a rendition of Faust.

He had cherubic black curls framing an elegant, pointed, and thoughtful face that seemed to belong to a man slightly older than me. The two of us reached the trees. I looked away from his face to see where Jennie had gone, but I turned back to the strange man when he spoke:

"Don't pay her any heed; your friend is just a coward."

"I know. She went on and on about leaving home to shack up with her older boyfriend and never did. There was some inadvertent wisdom in that, though." I looked into his eyes, which were focused intently on me. He offered me his arm, and I took it. We walked deeper into the woods.

"Now that we're together, I can tell you why I found you."

"Is it because your search was a success?"

"More than that. You've joined in a quest of your own."

"For the secret of will projection."

"I have to speak for you, as my father's most loyal bastard son. The power latches onto the mind, it digs out a place for itself. Soon enough, to live will be to hold dozens of bodies for oneself."

"Would you leave some of yourself in the puppets?"

"They would slowly fuse onto your mind. It will incorporate what sticks, until it no longer fits inside of your body alone. Then you must use it in order to keep your soul fast in your body; that is, unless you have done something that must not spare you death."

He ducked under a branch into a dark wall of brush; I followed him through the hedge. I stepped over a skeleton embedded in the threshold and into a ballroom lit by a sparkling chandelier. I looked down at myself to see that I'd gained an ornate Elizabethan gown in silk velvet. My skin glowed pale against the plush burgundy fabric.

I turned to my companion, who had gained a rainbow-sheened pearl on a gold chain. The same crowd that I vaguely recalled from my prom danced elegantly in an ordered choreography that had no place in my memory of them. He and I danced together.

I woke up confused. I got up and, after going to the bathroom and brushing my teeth, went downstairs to the kitchen. Victoria was already there. She held a steaming cup of tea that showed the cloudiness and wafted the scent of added blood. I sat down across from her and poured myself a cup with my usual, human, add-ins.

"Did it speak to you too?" I started up at Victoria for that comment.

"I did have an odd dream that claimed to know about the book, if that's what you're talking about."

"You know it is."

Anna took a moment before speaking, "A man in 16th-century German dress spoke for the book. It was odd; I don't know how I know this about him, but he was the son of Potestate's author. He was the last of his children to die. The legitimate ones preceded him into the pages: in killing the final progeny to finish the net for his own soul, he sealed his failure…"

Victoria picked up the thread, "The bastard fought back, mortally wounding our immortalist author, who was thus cut off from the means of binding his bodily and spiritual survival to that of the book. No ritual death, no soul capture."

"So now his sacrifices haunt his work," Anna's gaze fixed, staring through the kitchen cabinets, "I wish I knew the bastard son's name. He was far too beautiful to die like that." Victoria snorted. "I'm serious," Anna turned to face her, "He was stunning: black curls around a fair face, the manliest dorito torso."

"I do wish he'd gotten to live, at least long enough to make more of himself." Victoria sniggered and we went on to other topics. There was a hint of preoccupation about her, but Anna didn't press her about it.

When it came time to go to bed again, Anna hoped to see the bastard son again. She went to sleep, and woke up without having seen him. Over in the other room, Victoria had more luck. The ghostly woman had visited her again, and Victoria succumbed to the apparition's seduction.

Victoria followed it willingly, going deeper and deeper into union with the immortal wandering soul's figure. The author had not lived to see the success of his creation, his ready place yawned for a replacement. He would have looked upon the one set to conquer body after body before death claimed it with pride, or envy. I know not which.

Chapter 11

Beatrice Lovell stood before the squad. Her husband sat inconspicuously behind their semicircle, only here for her. "There's only one way we can escalate from here." The group waited for her to finish her thought, "I have to attack them directly with my magic." Before they could object, Beatrice continued, "It hasn't been enough to just use the daylight blades."

"Their potency against the vampires has two sources: the rare ore worked into the blade, and my will made manifest. The latter element can be far more efficiently directed if I were to join with you. I have found a way to resist the compulsion that the vampire Victoria possesses, and to extend the same protection to you all."

Kyle seemed to accept this announcement immediately. He had come to suspect this would happen when Mark came to enough to describe what happened when Victoria attempted to mind control him. It took magic to counter magic. "It's a large risk, exposing you to the fortunes of war, but it is the only proactive way we can escalate force. I expect you've written down the bladecasting process."

"It's in the fireproof safe, and another two safe places."

The spectre of death hovered around the room, as if it were summoned by the open discussion of this insurance policy for the fight against Beatrice's fall. It circled over the table, and fluttered out over Beatrice's head, with its choice none the wiser.

Oblivious, Kyle continued to speak, "Then we have safeguarded the future of our cause." This statement rippled out like a minor shock, and Martin felt the need to address the change in atmosphere.

"The specifics of our engagement need addressing," He wished his brother-in-law was less dramatic about the whole business. *It did wonders for getting people to join, but getting them this antsy right now, when we all need our wits about us, was counterproductive at best, and sabotaged our chances at worst.* "Now that we are agreed on its importance." *This was much easier when Mark Newbury was still with me; he understood the import of keeping the group under control.*

"We have six members and it's been more than a year since our friend and comrade Mark Newbury died; I congratulate his widow for her steadfastness in staying with us. The time has been spent preparing, but our enemy has had the same time to prepare as well. What I suggest is that we take stock of where we are now and how to realistically use Beatrice in a fight."

"She has none of our fighting strength and fifty time the magic of all of us combined."

"I know I belong in the rear," Beatrice's interruption brought every eye away from the plan to her, "It seems the rear must move forward." A misty look had clouded her eyes.

Kyle butted in: "Tris doesn't know what she's talking about. The closest she belongs to a pitched battle with what'll be an organized force is as far away as the blade activation teams usually are. Come on, it's time to think about what the vampires are going to do."

"They're gathering strength," was all Tris could manage to say in front of the others as she complacently allowed Kyle to lead her out of the room by the hand. When she was out of earshot he let her elaborate: "The vampire who escaped, she's joined the one who discredited Uncle Jim's prospect. Got him in jail for fraud. I miss him."

Kyle sat Beatrice down in bed; she stared vacantly out the window. "We're going to face an army. All I've done to be strong enough a magus, all I've lost in the process, it won't be enough to bolster us up to an advantage." Kyle sat down next to her. Ever since she'd been proven right in her insistence that Mark Newbury would die by the next vampire he attacked, he had put a greater stock by her ramblings when she was like this.

"I can't escape the end," Beatrice's eyes became intent, focused on something beyond sight, "I will face a force of vampires with preternatural powers like my own and I will meet my fate among them. I will die."

A suddenly as she started the episode, Beatrice closed her eyes and rubbed over them with her fingers. Blinking, she turned back to look on the here and now and noticed Kyle was there. "What happened?"

"You had another attack. This time you seemed to know who sent in those rocks to accuse Uncle Jim of salting the claim when he tried to get investors. You were also sure the same someone was the vampire our escapee joined to fight against us."

She rubbed her temples before speaking: "I don't remember any of this. Was I all morose and 'I have given up so much for the cause' again?"

"You were the same as every time. I think it's a side effect of all the work you've done to become clairvoyant enough to perfect the blades and find places to hunt. I think it's affected your mental stability. I think you should ground yourself for a few weeks, at least long enough to halt its progress."

"You didn't say I'd gotten worse. Also no, I won't give up keeping an eye in the sky for incoming threats to humanity. No way. Don't even try." Before he could mention the last thing she'd said under the influence of her psychic disassociation, Beatrice had gotten up and walked out of the room. She rejoined the meeting, excitedly announcing that 'the visions sucked ass' but they 'had told her to expect an organized vampire resistance'.

Beatrice was her usual confident, outgoing self, and everyone still in the meeting room couldn't help but react. The same people who had been hesitant of their chances before radiated the certainty of their strength and the inevitability of their victory. Kyle was left alone with the sinking feeling that nothing of the sort was bound to happen and that he was too much of a coward to undermine Beatrice's front and confront her with the prophecy of her own impending death.

"Our enemy leader is a stack of wet newspaper in all the best ways for us," I announced to anyone who might have wandered into the room while I spied on the Daylight Squad. Anna glanced up from her laptop. "Your screen's glow makes you look terrible." Anna shrugged back at me.

"I have a thesis project to edit and nowhere else is quiet."

"I've gotten the hang of astral projection."

"I can tell. How else would you be able to spy on them from here?"

"Your sarcasm can't take me down. I'm going to tell the others; they'll be happy." I started to get up, and as I readied my stiff limbs to go downstairs, Anna spoke again:

"How is Kyle weak?" Anna's attention was truly divided from her work. She stared at me, expecting an answer.

"He knows that Beatrice's persistent vampire-searching has made her quite attuned to seeing into the future because she predicted Mark Newbury's death. This type of prediction, unlike her usual, she makes in a trance, and it matches the book's description of the divine possession of the Sibyl. I'm almost fascinated enough to spare her for study, but I know survival is more important."

"How is that a weakness?"

"I'm getting there. Beatrice saw her own death, and Kyle won't look into it, or even try to keep her away from danger."

"I think this is a prediction of our victory." Anna just stared at me.

"Are they still talking?"

"They were when I popped out."

"Keep spying on them, then. Come back when you've found their battle plan." I snorted laughter at that.

"I thought you were against this: 'You might let them know you're there', and all that."

"Clearly you aren't giving yourself away, if they are still speaking their minds in front of you."

"You're funny, I'll get on going back." It took slightly longer to detach my mind from my body this time, Anna an ever-present distraction, but I made it back to the squad's 'secret' downtown meeting place.

I sat my invisible astral self on the windowsill. They were in a room on the second floor, above a storefront. The Daylight Squad had begun renting this apartment to hold their meetings since the isolated cottage had been compromised. I smiled to myself: *So much wasted effort and financial stress.*

The meeting had progressed to making solid plans. Beatrice effused friendly chatter, expertly guiding each member of the group to further the plan's production. It was fascinating to watch her, so manipulative in her means yet so genuine in her ends. I sat in awe, and took note of their next steps.

I floated out the window. The three-story downtown building was visible to me in its whole now. On the ground floor, a sketchy pawn shop faced the street; the floor above, the Daylight Squad moved on from plotting to socializing. I drifted through the wall into the third story to find out what was there.

There was a drug deal going on. I lost interest quickly.

I returned to my body to find Anna had returned to her manuscript. I spoke to her deliberately this time: "What do you think of them all as a group?" It was my turn to wait for Anna to answer a question.

"Besides what I've already said, my greatest impression is of the group's fragility. Individually, each of them is good enough, but the team fails to bring out the extra effectiveness one would expect from a team rather than an assortment of individuals."

"So?"

"Give them a real challenge and they'll break."

"You've said this before."

"It's my main impression, still."

"I'm gonna go share the results of my spying, come with?"

Anna shut her laptop. "Of course, I can't exclude myself from this." We walked downstairs separately looking for the others.

I pulled Theodora and Kento down from one of the rooms. Anna brought Miles and Ara across to us in the front room. Ira and Ara wandered in to see why everyone was gathering. The Sempronii were already there. The verandah's thick drape of ivy and lack of a glass half made this room the more private of the two rooms large enough for all of us.

"I have an announcement," I enunciated as clearly as I could, suddenly inspired by the enormity of what we had committed to do, "I have overheard via astral projection that Beatrice has foreseen where we will fight." I let the statement settle before I named the place: "It is just outside of their cottage in the countryside, the one they locked Anna and me in."

"I am also privy to their intended battle dispositions, which I am going to draw for everyone here once I find a pen and some paper." Anna pulled a pen out of the pocket of her sloppily-placed coat. I found a pad of paper in an end table drawer. "The reinforced squad will group around the building, keeping the magic-activators safe in the basement cell. They can't find an exact time for the confrontation, so they will tie themselves to the shelter to stay in peak condition"

"However, the surrounding woodlot has the high ground on the house on one side, and isolates it on three sides from a broad view of the surroundings. So long as we avoid the road immediately in front of it, as well as within earshot, we can remain concealed." I roughly sketched out what I was saying as I spoke, drawing the sightlines of the windows and the marking the positions of their watch.

"The only hint I got for timing is that it will take place at the crack of dawn sometime during the summer, after a dry spell. If it wasn't slowly driving her crazy, I'd envy Beatrice her clairvoyance." That last comment drew a derisive snort from Kento. I kept talking:

"I have countermeasures in mind:" Valentin came up from the post-hunt wash room just then. The conversation was reset to the beginning for him, and everyone took the opportunity to give their opinion now that I was silent and zoned-out.

Chapter 12

When the day finally came, Anna scanned the faces across the field. She saw at least a dozen people that she didn't recognize: the squad must have called in everyone they could. *Were they this desperate already?* "I would expect them to at least reserve a holding force in each squad's base area; they're making a stupid mistake. I think these are the members of all the squads in a day's drive from here."

Theodora's face was a mask, but the comments drew a muted laughter I could hear above the chorus of dawn cicadas. I glanced towards Victoria, but she was preoccupied keeping the puppets under control. They had the numbers, but we were superhuman. As far as I could tell, the split was about 5:2.

A hesitant look spread across their front line, one that drew a swift reaction: Kyle issued exhortations to them that were inaudible to me, but pushed them out from the only remotely defensible place, where they already were. They spread out from each other, drifting vaguely away from the cover of the obviously placed snipers on the upper floor of the building.

I squinted back at the upper window that had moments before been a well-framed shot of a sniper lazily sitting in position. The sun's growing presence and someone's wise decision to turn off the light in the room had washed out my view. All that was in the window now was the reflection of the rosy-fingered clouds above the trees. I had assumed there were others facing the other three directions, but this recent incompetence was making me doubt that.

I heard a thud behind me, and glanced to see that Kento had just stopped from running at his preternatural speed. He spoke to Theodora, but loudly enough that everyone huddled around could hear. "The back closest to the trees has a firewall. It incinerates whoever crosses it. I recognized it before I could trip it off. I suspect the walls have been impregnated with similar enchantments. There was telling ritual garbage in the dumpster."

"I don't think they could encircle the place completely, or why would they expose themselves at all?" Everyone turned to me at the sound of my voice.

"That much is obvious," Theodora took hold, "Victoria, you send in the drones first. Everyone else engage them next; who brought the crossbow?" Victoria raised her hand, which drew an assortment of unamused snorts. "You wait up in the bushes for a shot at the Sybil. Take a place away from me. I will be blocking their vampire repulsion psychically. Don't give me away."

We milled about for a few minutes until the plan was clear and everyone outside of our huddle was on the same page. The enemy stood out, their resolve buffered by Kyle's exhortations. Ira snarked at Victoria about her place out of the fray. Theodora gestured for me to approach her. I walked over.

When I got there, Theodora started giving me orders and drifting into shelter behind the crest of the hill: I was to stand by her while she blocked the Daylight blades' magic and break her distant focus in case of immediate threat. She sat down and presumably started to work her magic. I sat down next to her and wondered what would happen if our side were pushed back this far, where we were doubly blocked from the other side by the earth and the trees. I saw the people Victoria had taken for the occasion lurch past, towards where her spying had told her the magical activators would be.

The defenders hesitated to harm human beings, confused glances being exchanged even in the midst of mortal peril. They got past them, and Victoria's mind went with them. She could see through all three pairs of eyes: the homeless man she sent up to the second floor, the unkempt student on the first floor, and the dirty hippy sent into the basement. Victoria had no regrets for finding all the puppets randomly on the way here. The confusion was to our advantage.

She would tell me later: "I needed all my focus: I could feel the three minds ineffectively pull to regain control. When I found the magical weapon empowerment ceremony you had described, I had the random hippy stomp on the battery. I dropped my hold on the puppets. I hoped this would smoke the ever-important Beatrice out into the open from there. I saw her shock at the smashed battery through my puppet's eyes."

"The blocking Theodora was doing from behind me kept us on an even field with our opponent, but wouldn't get us in completely. From in my duffel bag, I pulled out my crossbow. I slung the bag over my shoulder and walked up to the bush I'd picked out at the top of the ridge. I slid beneath the lifeless branches of its forest-shaded side, ending up squatting with a view through the bush's vibrant, clearing-facing side."

"I set my bag, with its supply of spare bolts, at my elbow. I had to lean myself back on my left palm to do that without rustling the branches, so I immediately regretted not having placed the bag in ahead of me. I settled in to wait for my target, putting a bolt where it belonged and staring at the periphery of the building. It immediately felt like I'd been waiting there forever. The tide of the battle had been turned against the Daylight crew, but they held out better than I'd expect, given the Nightside's inherent advantages."

"Finally, I could see her. It had been a long enough wait crouched in the bushes, loaded crossbow cradled to my chest." Victoria unlocked the safety mechanism and took aim at Beatrice. She could see Beatrice's eyes on the ends of two of her psychic arms, seeking the interference with the vampire-binding compulsion embedded in the daylight blades. Her other arms were occupied keeping the daylight blades working. Before she could find her target, Victoria let loose.

The bolt hit its mark. Bright candy red blood gushed from the hole that it made in the front of her chest, trailing down the inside of her loose white dress. Beatrice Lovell fell, crumpled on the ground with the bolt almost completely through her body. Victoria whooped triumphantly.

Victoria couldn't stop laughing as the humans turned and fled. She chucked a few random bits of forest detritus after them, but they were ineffective weapons. "Was the rebel yell necessary?" Theodora called at Victoria.

"Very! The way they run is so indescribably satisfying, I have no words."

That drew a snort and a comment that Victoria found hilarious from Theodora: "It's bad luck, celebrating like a loser".

Part III
Chapter 1

After the aftermath, I sat in the back while Victoria drove and Theodora sat up front. The Sempronii sat on either side of me, cool to the excitement of the moment by long exposure to similar situations.

I bounced up and down in my seat like I did as a kid, running my hands over what I'd taken: the blonde curls shifted under my fingers as they slid over my actual hair. I stopped touching the captured scalp so it'd stay on. I broke out in giggles. Tertia glanced at me once before engaging: "Do you know whose that was?"

"She was Lilly White, not her real name, who I met once hanging around one of my 'vampire' interviews. We exchanged loaded pleasantries and I loved her hair. I didn't know she was one of them. Everyone else was looting so I took it." I couldn't resist hopping up and down in my terrible middle seat again: "I can't believe I'm alive and that built guy is dead, the one with the muscles. I never met him." I smacked my head on the roof of the car and let out a burst of laughter.

Undeterred, I kept bouncing: "I used to do this as a kid. It made my parents so mad. They told me it ruined the car's suspension but I didn't believe them. I still don't."

"I take it everyone else has done this before?"

Tertia spoke to me in measured words: "Everyone else here has indeed got to fight in a confrontation like this. It is inevitable to find oneself in these situations, given enough time. Time I have had in abundance, as have most of us."

"Victoria is the youngest of our group, who's only fought against hunters like this once before, if I'm up to date?"

Victoria took her cue to chime in: "Before this, I'd joined in a raid on a cult/hunter compound in the ass end of nowhere, Arizona, with Michael Burgher and his friend whose name I can't recall. Ira and

Valentin were there, I can't think who else, not Kento. They were much easier to kill, the cult members. They had none of the power of these Daylight warriors."

"They thought God was on their side," Theodora added, "which is the flimsiest paper shield of them all. No one knows the mind of God. Now none of them are left alive."

Gaius picked up the thread: "We live so long; it is inevitable that each of us will occasionally be enmeshed in the obligation to fight. Sometimes mere boredom is enough of a compulsion, if time has allowed it to become severe enough."

"Have you joined a war out of boredom?"

He smiled indulgently before he spoke: "Only the Napoleonic wars. I followed old Napoleon like a common prostitute, feeding undetected in the wake of the armies. I had rode out the revolution in our kind's deathly sleep, and once I had awoken I was aimless; it was the first thing I seriously thought to do."

"It was also the best thing I could have done, as hindsight has told me. I travelled over the whole of Europe, drank blood running hot and cold, and found several of my new friends. A higher-than-usual proportion of them have survived to the present. One of them is in the seat ahead of me."

I spared Theodora's reflection in the rearview mirror a glance at that, and turned back to Gaius before he could lose interest in regaling me. I was already too late. He had turned towards the window and fallen silent, absorbed in a memory. I don't know which.

I felt an urge to start going over my lump of actual loot, not just the increasingly regrettable scalp I was wearing. *So many things are gross now that my adrenaline is going down and I can think properly.* I would have pulled the thing off my head if I had somewhere that I wouldn't make gross to put it. My hair already needed to be washed. I looked over myself, noting the smears of dirt and blood on my clothes.

I could hear the Sempronii start talking over me about spending some time with Ara at their place after the Nightside members that weren't leaving immediately were in the coven house. This was their car, apparently. I disembarked with Victoria and Theodora, only noticing when Ara and Gaius passed me to get back in that we weren't at the coven house.

We were at the cottage Victoria had taken me to the day of our escape. I hadn't recognized the front way in, but that was where we were. I heard Theodora claim the first shower. I took a good look at my surroundings. The clearing and buildings hadn't changed much since I'd been here last. The full leaf of summer gave the place a more isolated feel, but everything was in the same place.

Victoria stretched out in the grass. I pulled the scalp off my head and wandered into the trees to dispose of it. Looking at the thing cold and sober, there was a surprising amount of fat on the inside. Unsurprisingly, it was now bloodless. I tossed the scalp on the ground where it wasn't immediately visible from the road or driveway. I hoped something would find it there and eat it.

Wandering back to the others, I saw that Theodora must have prodded Victoria's idleness, since she had retrieved the concealment supplies from the car. She was in the process of trading a pack of replacement clothes for a turn in the shower. Theodora walked over to me with a wad of bloodied clothes in hand: "Here's something else to go bury. I'll not contaminate myself with the spot, you'll wash later."

I took the bundle and wandered off in another direction, avoiding where I went on my first trip here. I pushed each piece individually under last year's moldering leaves. *Rot in peace.*

When I got back, Victoria was done and had set out a new outfit for me. I went to the shower, passing out the contaminated material through the mostly-closed bathroom door. Victoria went out to dispose of the stuff, and I closed it. It was time to drag the disgusting scalp grease out of my hair. I noticed so many trails of dried fluid that needed to go.

Chapter 2

Safe behind the pine and blackthorn hedges and a few weeks later, I
sat with Theodora and she opened the bottle. The wine darkened to
black from the pale, cloudy purple it showed as it poured when it
gathered to itself in the glasses. The sloes had been inedible raw, and
I was keen to find out if fermentation had improved them at all.

The wine tasted of regret. The lasting bitterness was only a mild
surprise: it did stick around. Theodora took my silence as an
invitation to begin a story that had the rehearsed air of one told many
times over.

"You remind me of someone I met briefly a long time ago. You were
both green as the first grass that splits last year's dead remains. He
couldn't have been older than sixteen. He stood with the other
privates, and they cajolingly mocked him until he approached me."

"I had been standing near what used to be my husband's barn, but
was then a burned-out husk. I surmised he was the only one of them
who spoke any French, seeing as their unit had joined Napoleon in
hopes of buying a nation-state with their blood."

"The young man proceeded to awkwardly proposition me: sex in
exchange for some canned food he ever-insistently waved at me. The
rest of the lot looked on, searching for material for future jabs and
resisting laughter. Maybe they were looking for something else, I
don't understand Polish."

"I gestured that he follow me behind a still-standing section of wall to
complete the exchange, and with a sheepish look of disbelief he came
along. Out of sight of the others, he started to pull off his uniform
haphazardly. I turned away and made as if I were unbuttoning my
blouse, but instead pulled the dagger I had for this very situation out
of hiding."

"He was the one to get penetrated. I sent the edge deep into his
viscera, ending him in an outpouring of blood from his guts."

"Once I was sure he was dead, I stuck a hand out from behind the wall. I called out to the rest of them, promising them an opportunity to make fun of their all-too-brief friend. I had to resort to mocking sound effects to lure one of them in."

"Maybe they were looking to take the can away and laugh at my reaction, I don't know."

"I did manage to slit the next one over's throat before he could usefully react to the first's corpse, but he was followed by three more, who I couldn't handle all at once. I got the closest one to me in the face before the farthest squeezed off a shot. It hit me in the kidney."

"I was overwhelmed by lust for the kill; I laughed at their bullets and abused them with words they couldn't understand. The final uninjured one shot at my heart, hitting me in my left lung. That put a stop to my words."

"The next thing I know I've woken up as what I am today. My maker had been impressed by me and thought I would do well as one of his kind. Gaius Cassius Sempronius and I stalked Napoleon's army all the way back on its retreat, then wherever it went until his final defeat."

"Blood ran hot and cold, and my maker and I feasted." Theodora looked lost in thought for a moment, but before I could cut in with a question she started up again: "Someone who claimed to be the Duke of Wellington's body servant tried to bum some boot polish off me, but he wasn't well-dressed enough, so I called him out. The attention made him run away, so it was probably a pretext to get close to me for something shameful." A smug smile creeped over Theodora's face as she recalled the memory. I finally got a word in:

"I call shenanigans on you: what bullets leave you still capable of going on like that? Two shots and you're still strong enough to make the change? Fake!" I was propelled to speak louder and faster in anticipation of being cut off. Theodora laughed at me. She pulled off her tank top.

I could see two scars on her front: clearly gunshot wounds. One was over her left kidney, the other was in her lung a good inch astray of the lowest point of her heart. I looked around to her back, "The kidney one is a through-and-through, but there's no way you could have survived the other shot. It must have bounced off the inside of one of your ribs, I don't see an exit wound anywhere."

I crawled around the grass to see the rest of her: "You definitely should be dead from this." That comment brought out even more mirth from her:

"I'm two hundred and twenty-one. Of course I should be dead."

"What's really shocking is how long I'd been picking off those damnable locusts before I met the wrong end of a firing squad like that. I'd already collected a heap of their bayonets in my basement. I hadn't yet graduated to collecting severed penises."

When I didn't react, she went on: "It's a joke; it was severed dicks I collected all along."

I was at a loss for words again: "Is that also a joke?" Apparently my confusion was the joke, since Theodora laughed, her face lit by an almost angelic smile.

"I started a hoard of my torn-out hair," It was about time I had something to say, "I pulled at it in stress, and I thought I had to keep it to keep the vitality I'd lost. It wasn't enough to get me into med school, anyway. I'd been on that since I had any plan for what to do as an adult. I'd grow up and become a doctor."

"I don't have any other experience even remotely like yours, except coming into knowledge of the supernatural."

"I get less relatable every year," Theodora continued, "I have already outlived the generation of my great-grandchildren as they died in old age. I first thought I'd die in childbirth or of some disease, then I thought I'd die by the invader or starve. I was sort of right. I came back from the dead, and now I've drifted further away from my time than I ever thought was possible."

"I wonder if there's any point to me living on like this and not anyone who would do more for the world. I've never had any taste for go-getting or whatever it's called now. I stand like a tower in the middle of a plain, the strength and refuge of a soul. I sometimes think about turning someone who would keep going and get some progress, so death need not end their work."

"In the end, I always change my mind. I wonder if I would end up ruining whatever drove them by turning them, those faraway do-gooders, and leave the world worse for the loss of the rest of their life's work. A few weeks ago, I thought about my place in the world again. I remembered the sort of people I thought were changing the world for the better and considered offering an eternity; I recalled the people who actually improved the world in the same time. I thought of the people I'd admired on principles I no longer hold."

"I've become disenchanted with the idea of bettering the world lately, as the implications of this line of thought set it. Even if I can make more like what I value, those ideals will inevitably change and I will be left with a world still divorced from perfection."

"This pointlessness has become apparent to me. As surely as the gurgled last words of that green boy were doubly incomprehensible to me, we will all end alone and unremembered once the world has died, the sun exploded, and humanity is no more."

"Victoria goes on about flying away in a rocket ship before the world dies, but I'd like to die with my world if I ever live long enough to see it happen."

"It makes me think of the present. I have once again been the innocent's initiator into the weight of life-or-death consequence. Those children had no idea what they were in. I've been a vulture on the field of battle so many times, I've seen the same transformation."

"I can still see the bloody corpse of that young man as I did when I wandered over a newly-made monster. The dingy brown hair, layer of dirt over his babyface, the maw of his mortal wound; it all seemed so much more real. I could see, smell, feel so much more of him with my reborn body. Of myself, I felt as if I were at the end of a long tunnel from my body and wrapped in cloth."

"I have never felt so strongly as I did when I was human. I wish I could lie in the grass and feel again, even if I could only feel my final moments on the ground before I was turned. I wouldn't regret dying there. I had done everything I humanly could against my enemy. The rest of my life was solidly out of my control at that point."

"Do you ever miss your past self?"

I had to pull myself together to answer: "I miss my old optimism. I used to feel so secure giving my all to things, knowing I would probably succeed. I was a very sincere child."

"She doesn't like what my guile has made of me, my inner child. I would love to become her again; I know I can't."

"There is no cure for the longing to unite with your better self." Theodora's final response stuck with me.

That night, I sat on the grass with my friend by my side, under a clear, still, and warm sky. I admired her when I wasn't preoccupied by engaging with her speech. I loved her for her passionate defense of her land and her pride. I saw an efficacy and a strength in her I wanted for myself. These are feelings I admit to myself. I felt them purely in the moment, and ironically when I thereafter recalled them.

I sat there in the open with my bitter drink. The glow of the moon reflected off my companion's ethereal-perfect skin. I admired the deep burgundy, covered by black lace bra that I couldn't pull off. I found the moon full above my head. When I looked back down Theodora was looking at me.

"I couldn't pull off that colour, and since I can't think of anything serious to say, that's what I said." *I should shut up now.* Theodora blinked at me.

"I think you and Victoria are made for each other."

Chapter 3

How do I begin this section? What should I admit? The enormity of
what I was doing sat heavy on my head. My first deadline was long
past and I searched for a job as a new PhD. *No book, no royalties.* I
thought back to those days, what I knew had been going on where I
wasn't. *Whose side should I put myself on or how should I account
for my defection?* I pushed myself to keep writing, despite what I'd
forgot, despite what I didn't or couldn't know:

It had saved my life, I thought, I insisted to myself that Victoria's
power had been the only thing between myself and indefinite evils.
The feeling that this was a compromise I couldn't live with still
dogged me. I threw myself into my work, but even with the chaos that
was my life slowing me down, there wasn't enough thesis writing to
keep me distracted from my moral inquietude.

Despite its value to my final confrontation, I didn't want to improve
my bond with Victoria Falls anymore. I felt conflicted about my
purpose, and didn't want to sink into complacency with her. *These
words on the page still haunt me. I wish I could have found a better
way to put this.*

I had to break it off with Victoria. Every day she found new ways to
abuse her power, or reused old ones. None of the other vampires saw
fit to try and stop her, since she was so clever about maintaining
secrecy. I still feel for her, though. *I almost wish I could just be o.k.
with her myriad abuses.*

But still…

I finally made the commitment. I went into the file of emails that I
kept for if I ever needed to contact someone again, but couldn't stand
to be reminded of them by seeing them in my contacts or inbox. I
found the email from Kyle that gave me the contact info of his two
immediate subordinates: the late Mark Newbury and the still-living
Martin Lovett.

The message sat unwritten, with only a subject line to its name for hours. I paced in my familiar manner, with my laptop open to a blank wall free of reflective surfaces that my non-message was safe to stand exposed to. I finally did find the resolve to type what I ended up sending Martin Lovett, under the subject "Change of Heart".

Martin Lovett,

We met once before it all went to hell by that promotion party. I regret that I had to take the other side against you in the most recent confrontation. Beatrice was a gem of humanity, which was lessened by her shattering. I present you with my condolences, knowing full well that I am one of the last people you ought to accept them from.

I hope this message finds you doing as well as you can. You have lost someone more dear to you than any in my life. I had been shocked at your reaction to me at the capture of Victoria, so I took her protection against you. This decision has proved shortsighted.

Victoria has taken to herself at least a dozen people, whom she puppets to various ends. Some of them she feeds on, some do chores, sometimes she just uses her control of one of their bodies to rape them. I did try and talk her down in the beginning, but now I believe that the extra bodies are necessary for her to stay alive.

It pains me to say it, since I ought to be grateful for the way she was to me, but Victoria Falls needs to die. The other vampires are no help, since she is a canny secret-keeper; common humanity is none the wiser to her depraved acts. I offer what I've learned about her to you so we can accomplish this goal. Let us rid the world of her menace.
Anna Carlson.

The response I got was through a forwarded copy of the message. Norah was the one who wrote the response:

Anna,

You left us with quite a few questions, ones that need to be resolved before you can join back. It is no surprise, I assume, to hear that our operation has lost most of its support. The fact that we had never been defeated was a huge draw for members before the dread occurrence happened.

The two Blackwells have not been heard from since, and they're not alone. Our professor Meyers, and most of the satellite squad members, have deserted. I'd be transparently lying if I didn't admit to some desperation for help right now. We, too, noticed the effect of Victoria's power in battle and we've been preparing to take her out.

As much as both Martin and I mistrust you, we have decided that it's time the flaking benefitted rather than harmed us. Meet us back where you met Beatrice and Martin for the first time.

Norah Alghaul.

I stared at the messages. *It's done. I've betrayed my savior to the threat to my life. It's time for me to go kill myself.* But of course I'm not going to do that, I'm going to put down the monster that damnable cult made when they started systematically going after vampires. *Without the Daylight Squads, Victoria would never have had the initiative to learn how to puppet.*

I wondered if I would ever get to keep an easygoing friend. My sister got married and stopped hanging out with me, my boyfriend Bane's stupidity wore on me, and now my savior and friend has slid into decadent evil with mind control powers.

I still don't know how to feel about this part. No matter how I edit it, it always feels too personal, like I was baring my soul to every fat, maladjusted troll with access to my book if I left them in. If I cut my feelings, then my change from the Nightside to the remains of the

Daylight Squad wouldn't make any sense. *Unless I cut the reference to my joining the Nightside and pretended to have been undercover for the Daylight Squad.*

It was almost enough to make me nostalgic for when my moral dilemma was between loyalty to a friend and loyalty to my principle, nice and external. What I tackled now was the sort of a problem had no good solution. I glanced at the clock in the corner of my screen. *It's time for work.* Dr. Brockmann's addiction study wasn't going to administer itself. I set aside my manuscript and got going.

Chapter 4

It was an elusive, airy thing she lacked, this love of mine.

I too had fled the scene, met by flying pieces of stone and moss and wood. I would have run if not for my burden, my love. Norah was the only one left when I made it to the cars. She stayed for me, and I stayed for her. I hefted the body into the centre of the back seat and got in after her. Norah drove away.

She pulled up to my brother-in-law's house, where we had run the squads from before the demon escaped her capture. Surrounded by neighbours, we could rest confident that they won't try another all-out assault. Not while their secrecy could be broken so easily, at least. Norah pulled into the garage, and was both my director and assistant in bringing the body into the basement. I settled myself in the spare bedroom we'd used, my love and I, when we were over.

I could hear her steps towards the basement door, which she closed behind her with a firm thump. I sat with my uncomprehending grief for Beatrice. *That's the way Martin Lovett likely came home. It would have been different for Norah:*

With each step down, Norah felt a stronger pull. At the bottom of the stairs, she found what was calling her. The spirit of Beatrice Lovell was seated next to her lifeless body. She smiled at me, and raised her left hand to the still-bright blood on her ghostly dress: "I didn't expect to see you again so soon."

I stared in disbelief for a moment before summoning the sense to speak, "Why are you here?"

The ghost of my friend's smile widened, radiating a spirit of cruelty, "I've come to help you avenge my death."

Before I could respond to her in any way, Beatrice cut in again, "I've seen the path to my killer's death, Norah. It's so clear from this side. You'll need my magic for it."

"What?"

"Let me finish, Norah. My right ulna and left radius, take them, you'll need them." I glanced behind me at the foot of the stairs. She wasn't talking to a Norah behind me. When I glanced back, Beatrice had popped right in front of me.

"Norah, my friend, you've been the best help to me." The ghost's face contorted into a familiar expression: the insistent one Beatrice used when she really wanted something. "I know that with the use of my power, you'll be able to defeat the vampire Victoria. You just need to salvage it from my body.

It was just like her to push like this, just like me to do what I'll do next. "Fine," the ghost was elated, making the same full-faced look of delight Beatrice used to at my acquiescence, "What do I need the bones for?"

"You're making a pair of wands, one for you and the other for Anna. She'll change her mind about Victoria soon. I can hear her angsting about it, all: 'can I put up with her sins against free will?' and 'can I really betray my friend for my principle?' She's really a tiresome woman, especially knowing the outcome."

I can't say I was OK with it, but I followed Beatrice's detailed instructions to capture the magical essence still left in her body. The two arm bones she specified were set aside for working while I got a few sacks of driveway salt at the hardware store. I packed her corpse into the broken chest freezer with the salt, and shut the lid.

Beatrice cheerfully surveyed my work, and sat down next to me as I carved her bones into wands. At her insistence, I finished the carving before I took a can of bleach to the bloodstains trailing from the garage to the body's final resting place in the chest freezer. It took far more than I'd expected, and at the end of it all I'd been awake for twenty-five hours and been through more than I'd ever been in so short a time. Despite my exhaustion, I still needed to shower before I slept.

In the morning, Beatrice's ghost was still there. I turned to the clock on Kyle's nightstand and saw that it was three in the afternoon. She laughed at me, drawing my eyes back to her. "You're so shocked," Beatrice stifled some more chuckles, "sleeping in my brother's bed and stunned when I'm interested."

Beatrice got up off the edge of the mattress and started pacing. I spoke faintly: "He's too dead to care," the ghost was immediately blocking my entire field of vision, and I started. She stared me down for an agonizing moment before speaking:

"I know you're new to this, but you can't say things like that." Blood started to drip from her mouth, "You have to do what I say, and get revenge. You live; Victoria Falls dies. That's it."

At the end of that word, Beatrice was gone in just as disorienting a fashion as she had approached me. She would return at random intervals: telling me to order some lead sheeting online, how to make it into an insulating shield wrapping, and to mind my mouth over what it was for.

Beatrice told me secrets about how to shield a mortal from a would-be immortal's supernatural powers, guiding me through making three wands out of blackthorn, and three charms against mind control.

I struggled to keep up with the bills attached to this place, even though I got rid of my own. Martin was no help. He just sat in the computer chair in the guest room, staring at his laptop, but not doing anything useful with it. Beatrice wouldn't allow me to intervene in any way, so I left him to his vacant, forlorn gaze and morose thoughts:

In the present, there is little I can do. I found myself alone with Norah in the aftermath of the sound defeat we had been dealt. The Daylight Army was done: now that the good-time adventurers were gone, we lacked the numbers to form viable squads.

Kyle had rushed at them at the sight of the corpse, and that had made him into the same. Everyone ran after that; death had claimed both the people that had a claim of group leadership: Captain Daylight himself and his Sibyl. In the weeks immediately following that scattering, I felt numb.

I spent hours and days immured in idle grieving. I sat inside the wall, peering sightlessly at Norah's rituals from my computer chair, lacking the focus and drive to even try to get the others back or find another way to keep us protected from reprisal.

A month and a half after the loss I could finally face Norah again. It was out of necessity rather than choice. I sent it over to her. I couldn't even bring myself to open it.

That's how it must have happened, if my thoughts are correct. Anna got off the bus at her stop. *I can't tell: this is the best I can reconstruct, so it's going in the book. I don't care anymore. I have to finish it, no matter how late.*

Taking another look at my manuscript after work, I regretted everything I'd ever deleted again. *I don't know how to fit my actual experience to my public face. 'Lillianne Knight' might have joined the Daylight Squad, but never the Nightside.* I resigned myself to going over the whole thing again. *I can't even tell how much of everyone else's stuff I made up anymore.*

Chapter 5

The time had come. It had been nigh for awhile now, but it was here.
I had been accepted. As I knelt, praying once more to be cleansed of
my innumerable sins, I saw a light begin to glow from the ceiling. It
grew stronger over the hours, and I felt certain that it was a divine
presence making itself known to me.

I thought over my former life. With my love, I lived above a mass of
humanity; they worked our mine, and feed us with their blood. It fell
to me to keep the overseers to their promises of secrecy, and to him to
hold the rest under us. When it came time for us to flee the
arrangement's inevitable collapse, the two of us massacred the
encampment behind us.

The worst slaves were first, then came a round of isolation so none
could come to the rest's rescue. My husband and I proceeded then to
play them off each other, keeping our servants close until the end. It
was a masterpiece of cruel manipulation. We walked out from the
place after a century of entrenchment; I was haunted by the means.

The same must have tormented him, or perhaps something obscure to
me, for within another fifty years he took his own life. I remembered
the despair and sentimental attraction I'd felt as I drifted towards and
away from my past. The mine, my love's final resting place, and the
vast waste formed a Bermuda's triangle that kept me trapped within.

A light seemed to emanate from where the Godhead would have been
in the chapel fresco of my childhood, had it been hidden behind the
featureless wall in front of me. Perfect love washed over me, and my
memory took a new cast, although another of my crimes came to
mind.

I had been drifting over the desert like a tumbleweed, tossed back and
forth across the same stretches. Over a familiar mesa I climbed,
seeing a distant campfire from my new vantage. The shadows of men
flitted across the fire. I wondered what they were doing this far in the
wilderness. This wasteland had nothing to hunt, and naturally did not
support either pastoralism or agriculture.

I moved as swiftly as the wind, approaching the camp in moments. Within earshot, I settled in the shadows and listened. They had robbed a landowner one of them had a grievance with, and they were on the way to Mexico. From the way they spoke of their route in the morning, I could tell they were going in the wrong direction.

The desparados broke camp at dawn, and I waited for them beyond a blind bend in their path. I was a wild-looking thing then, my mourning dress faded and hair escaping its coif in delicate strands. The three of them were shocked, and I smiled as I approached them. "You gentlemen have come to the right place, I've been waiting up for you all night."

The first man I reached became my first meal in a year. The second I had to chase down on foot, for the third I had to catch up to his horse. I know I overheard their names but, try as I might, I cannot recall them. *I am not and cannot be worthy of grace; there are sins I have that I do not know and cannot atone for.* I felt the realization settle: it is beyond my power to make the offer, I can only do as I did after then, turn towards the light and life of civilization. I turned towards God.

The light before me took shape. It was a glowing skeleton in a dress that I recognized all too well. I had worn it the day I met my beloved, the false immortal who turned me from my path. **He offered you a place away from me, you took it.**

The apparition spoke without opposition. I and she were one, and her voice rose from my heart. *I knew this separation was an illusion.* I could not bring myself to speak with the words of my mouth. I could feel the air sluggishly circulate within me: so much had rotted away, but so much more of me shone brilliantly above.

I have come to bring you to me. I felt a wave of warm, creamy light washed out of me, lapping at the walls. The edges of my vision blurred into white. Tears dripped cool tracks down my flesh. I bid it farewell.

This Golden Haze

The fields were silent; the trees blew in the wind, but not a thing hit hard. Whether I sat or stood, I felt perfectly at ease. The sun gently sank in the East, and it cast a soft golden light into the fog that thinly covered the landscape.

The land shimmered, bleeding into a forest, like a *fata morgana* coming to life. I followed the stream as it flowed uphill, seeking the marvel to which it was drawn. I approached a sheer face and stepped through the waterfall to find myself atop the cliff.

Over the edge, the world was thrown into a sharp, glittering relief. The trees' every needle and every leaf was distinguishable, one from the other. The light shone off of them where the sun's rays caught them; precious few points reached me. They were a light, warm yellow.

The wind slightly brushed my hair back from my face. It eased me perfectly, my body felt with the landscape. It glowed with a cool heat that kept me as comfortable in myself as if I were immersed in completely clear, breathable water.

I felt this way until the perfection was broken by a sensation: I could feel a hollow weight build in my stomach. It settled into my womb. I stood there, and I felt myself shred into two halves; the falseness overwhelmed me.

Chapter 7

I stood awkwardly around the table with the other two. We were left together with the former Daylight Army's mission narrowed to one focus: defeat the power-mad vampire Victoria. Norah's eyes drifted around the room. Martin glared at me. Before I could finally break the tension with actual speech, Norah did:

"What's going on over there?"

Not the best choice to defuse the tension, but it needs to be said. "Victoria Falls is melting down. She's become obsessed with developing her skill at overwhelming the willpower of people and controlling them like her puppet."

"To that end, she has taken to living in a cottage with a set of people with which she amuses herself. Victoria's covenmates, the Nightside, have committed to a policy of noninterference. So long as Victoria keeps the secret of her kind's existence, she can do whatever she wants with the puppets."

Martin spoke: "What about the specific things you mentioned in the message?"

"Victoria's taken to making them do chores and amuse her, sexually or otherwise. There was a fight club for awhile, but she got bored of that quickly. The rest of her coven insisted she leave with them for the countryside to keep their kind's secrecy. The abnormal behavior of the puppets would draw hunters and possible exposure to regularly-within-eyesight citizens, they said, and none of them wanted to be caught by her mistake."

"That was her coven's consensus when I cut off my relationship with them. I found that unacceptable. I had to do something to stop her. I have to actually do something."

Martin nodded at me; Norah continued ask questions: "Who fought against us? We had Beatrice's warning, but no idea that so many of you could mass like that."

I used one of the responses I'd thought of before I committed to this: "Once a vampire has reached a certain age, there are few of its kind they are not somehow connected to. The ones you faced included the lovers and longtime friends of the vampires you'd killed up to that point, as well as some habitual hunter-killers."

"There had already been a concerted effort among the vampires to discover who was picking them off and how to stop them. When Victoria and I escaped, we brought with us knowledge of the Daylight Squads and speculation about how to defeat them. I had been set against you, and I felt obliged to support the other side in exchange for their protection."

"There are quite a few hardened veterans among them. I got to hear some of their horrible experiences; you were no match for them as fighters."

"There are habitual hunters of vampire slayers?" *What a thing to pick out from all that.* I answered:

"There are. Some vampires develop a habit of killing or otherwise incapacitating human vampire hunters. There is an equilibrium between vampires, hunters, and ordinary humans that lets us all live the status quo. One of these I met has had a grudge against hunters from four hundred years ago, when one killed his maker. He lost his arm in a tsunami attempting to drag the grudge-maker in through a window."

"He literally lost the arm and couldn't find it again. I don't think it's out there anymore."

"So it's a thing for vampires," Norah cut me off.

"It is." I looked after her glance to the empty space behind Martin's left shoulder. He hadn't moved. My eyes returned to Norah, who had noticed my flicker of attention. She asked another question: "What did you do for them?" *A hard one now.*

"I was a few things for them: I was an ear for their experiences, a confessor for their sins, a link to the present, and a prop to look less suspicious. I think some of them just liked me as a person."

"I have to admit I came to like some of them, too. I got to be regaled about the Napoleon's failed invasion of Russia, the Forty Years War, and the Civil War, the American one. They were all in a slightly unhinged style that betrayed years of obsession." I was losing my audience.

"I let them ramble and looked normal in public. Do you have anything else to ask?" They glanced at each other, and Martin spoke: "How are you as a fighter?"

"Pretty bad. I haven't practiced anything since I quit karate in tenth grade." Martin grimaced:

"What, did your parents stop making you?"

It was meant as a sarcastic joke, but I answered seriously: "You got it; they did. I was never properly engaged in it. It felt like I was always either frustrated by doing poorly or bored with repeating things I already did well. That was my problem with all athletics, I never took to any of it."

"Have you ever handled a gun?"

"Nope, never."

"How long ago was tenth grade?"

I counted off the years on my fingers: "It's been twelve years." *Damn, I've gotten old.*

"You'll need to work on it a lot then," I caught a glimpse of purpose in Martin, "and I'm the one in a position to get you ready. Norah has magic to see to." *I'm going to hate this like I hated taking karate.*

"The time to deny your help is long gone." The conversation went on along the same lines. The two of them seemed to grow to trust me more even over the conversation. *At least enough for this to succeed.* I felt a tug of regret. *I'll really have to undertake a transformation, now that I'm committed.*

I found a new daily routine. There was a cloud of tension around the house. I paid rent, did basic housework, and practiced martial arts. Occasionally, some petty annoyance set off the latent tension between me and the other two. I had liked the Nightside better, but now I was on the side of the Angels.

"The blackthorn is a wall of daggers: one of them is here in this wand," Norah handed it to me. The wand looked for all the world to be a completely normal smoothed wooden rod. I don't know why one would normally own such a thing, but it didn't glow or radiate energy. It was an ordinary stick of blackthorn wood.

"What do I do with it?"

"You direct your will at your adversary with it." *So I'll have to stab them in the eye with it, then; no improvement over a regular stick.*

"I have some exercise to do now. Martin is on my case. Any special way to store this?" Norah looked to the empty air over my shoulder before answering:

"No. Just put it wherever." I nodded my comprehension, turned, and left. *I think she's taking orders from a ghost.* The next few days confirmed my suspicion. Her gaze focused on empty space, which she nodded and gestured at when she didn't think I was looking. I even caught her speaking to an empty room once when I left the shower running to go get a new bar of soap from the absurd stockpile in the laundry room. Norah was interacting with someone that I couldn't see.

I racked my brain for what exactly Beatrice had said about her magic, finding nothing about gaining information, or anything else, from spirits. Every vague allusion pointed to astrological timing being important, 'drawing the star's nature down into a suitable earthly vessel' was what Beatrice had said about her own magic, *I think that's what she said, at least. I was so preoccupied with anticipation.*

If I assume that magic is real then the way Beatrice had reacted to Maria Cortés, and her escort's reaction was significant. Beatrice must have expected to be fine in front of her, or she would've delegated the responsibility to Martin and Kyle. They had seemed surprised at her reaction at the time. After that, Beatrice was never on the scene near a vampire until the end.

If Beatrice had been accustomed to a greater role in the touchy-feely stage of the investigations, then her vulnerability to the presence of vampires must have been acquired. I wonder what the effect of channeling the energy for the blades through herself and, "in an act that was the exact opposite to a vampire's feeding, pouring the celestial magic into its metal body" was.

I remembered stifling a sarcastic quip at Beatrice's characterization of the blade as the inversion of its target. *I've forgotten the joke though; it must not have been that clever.*

Pulling myself back to the present, I found had arrived at an inevitable-seeming conclusion: Beatrice must have, perhaps inadvertently, made herself into something more than human, and was now haunting her former follower. I looked around the room. It was blandly-furnished and neat as always. The recent myopic focus of everyone here showed in a layer of dust and general uncleanliness, but there was no otherworldly presence I could detect.

Is she stalking me or Norah? I can't believe that Beatrice harbored any good feeling for me: I had left her side and fought on the Nightside in the battle that killed her. The feeling that something disembodied was present followed me from that moment on. I went about daily life, editing my project and running each whole iteration by the Birdman. I practiced fighting techniques with a barely-present or sullenly there Martin.

An intent began to build in me. I would get to the bottom of this ghost. If it was in fact what remained of Beatrice Lovell, it may be in it for revenge: against Victoria, who actually killed her, but possibly also against me. There were so many ways for the fortunes of this hunt to turn so that both me and my opponent joined the dead.

I started to examine the rooms differently. I had already seen everything above grade, beneath it the basement was broken into two rooms: a finished workroom and an unfinished storage room. The stairs led into the unfinished section, which had a spare fridge and chest freezer conveniently set at its base. The workroom was tiny and transparently full of Beatrice's old occult supplies. Norah was using it now and nothing seemed to be out of place or hiding anything.

I searched through all the opaque plastic totes of stuff that filled the storage area, one by one when everyone else was out. All I found was evidence of a few hobbies that had gone by the wayside, some used childhood clothes, and old photo albums. After I'd searched the last tote, I decided to check the chest freezer for ice cream. After all, it may have been forgotten about in the basement. I dropped the lid as soon as I glimpsed the contents of the freezer.

I opened it again to confirm what I'd seen. There was a mummy packed in salt in the chest freezer. I couldn't recognize its face, but it wore the clothes Beatrice had died in and her platinum-streaked pixie cut. Nothing that I could make sense of said it wasn't Beatrice. I shut the lid again.

Crap. I've found exactly what I was looking for. It's definitely Beatrice's ghost informing Norah. I stood there for a moment, waiting for my mind to accept the facts that battered at it through my eyes. *Norah had taken away and hid Beatrice's body while we were looting. Somehow this is letting Beatrice's ghost interact with her. What in hell did she do to herself?*

I reopened the freezer. I noticed that it wasn't cold this time. I pulled on the cord and found it plugged into the wall, not an extension cord, so the freezer itself must be broken. I got back to the body. *I wonder how much I can mess with it with no one noticing. Has Norah kept it here to be here or is she doing something to it?* I shut the door and walked away before either of them could walk in on me.

I went upstairs to find Martin already back from his arms deal. "The stuff is in the garage," he barked in lieu of a greeting. I made an affirmative sound to show I understood. "You disapprove, college?"

"I don't like the liability. We're set between two dangers: what I presume are illegal firearms and the aftermath of the battle drawing the authorities to us, and the monster herself. I doubt either of our feelings have any weight, anyway. The lines have been drawn and our fate is sealed."

It was Martin's turn to snort, but I kept talking, mostly to myself: "Both humanity and the monster stand at either of our sides, ready to crush us between them. Vampirekind in general has consented to let Victoria's madness run its course, so long as it remains secret. Our challenge on that side is just Victoria and her puppets. On the other side, the massacre in the countryside has attracted police and media attention. I can't say what the authorities know well enough to connect or to act on. Nothing like that has been reported publicly."

"For all I know, the authorities could be in on the secret," I continued. Glancing towards my audience, I found Martin inattentive.

"I just spent the last of our money," He spoke still staring to the left of my face.

"Then our armaments are at their peak, or are you thinking of something else?"

He faced me and said, "What do you think I can do?"

"I don't know what you can do."

He sat looking stonefaced at me for a moment. "You need practice. There's no way you can just pick this up and use it even remotely close to well." Martin punctuated his comment by standing up and leading me out to the gun. At least I assume that was the point of him getting up and going to the garage so abruptly.

I followed him in. He pulled a tarp off of a new lump of stuff. It hid a pair of automatic rifles and a crate of ammo. "This is somehow what I expected," I said, since the situation really did call for a response, and Martin was silent. I squatted down, "so little and so much for all that money." The crate was labelled as holding 2000 rounds. "Is the signage accurate?" I looked up at Martin, who had been staring at me intently.

"No shock?"

What an odd response. "We're beyond shock at the reality of having to fight for ourselves right now, don't you think? We have both already seen this."

"It won't be the same."

"Is anything ever the same?"

The Madness of Victoria Falls

I could feel through them all. All of the minds I had grasped and held to myself.

In my leftmost hand, I held a beautiful man. He had a body that fit my ideal completely. I held him for my pleasure and my whims. In my middle left, a strong man with bad teeth was finishing taking out the wall between the bedroom and main room. I could feel his exertion, his pain when my attention drifted and he fucked up his task.

In my centre left was the greasy pedophile. I'd picked him as someone who wouldn't be missed enough to be reported missing. I'd needed more free labor. Now his thoughts, his unnatural lust, flitted around my brain. Should he die, the whole of it would stick to me, that much I knew. My skin crawled with disgust. I regretted this.

I held myself at the core. My hair puffed up with tangles. I'd meant to get one of the puppets to see to it for days, now, it seemed. I went ahead and got bad teeth to comb it, pulling him away from his task. I leaned back, feeling the hunger's drain on my strength. I knew I'd feel the weakness of blood loss if I fed off one of them. If one of them died, I'd gain another ghost flapping about my head. The first puppet to die's neurotic fear of cobwebs flapped around my ears. I screamed at them all: *get to work!*

In my centre right, I held a beautiful woman. She hated me under my compulsion. The others did too, most of them. I choked her will again, feeling it weaken, but having to shift my strength over the rest before it fully died again. All of them needed to be contained, all. The effort it took to keep everyone in hand was consuming me. I ran and ran, spiraling towards and away from myself.

In the grasp of my middle right hand stood my lowkey errand girl. She was ugly: not as hideous as the strong man or greasy pedo, but a lowkey ugly the same. She walked unnoticed, and I sent her to go for things. She never really left, though, the other place was as present as where I stayed. I could feel her deep-seated longing to break her invisibility. It latched onto my fear of irrelevance and rooted into my mind. In my rightmost hand, I held a neurotic whom I held by her fixations.

The bodies all had things to say to me: they needed to be fed, washed, and otherwise cared for. I took in exchange whatever I wanted from them. It would have been fitting for me to say that I loved to take care of them, but I didn't. If I could, I would kill all of them to be rid of them. Their feelings were too rooted into my mind, I wouldn't be rid of them if they died.

The beautiful lovers felt contaminated by my touch; I felt contaminated by their feelings. The disgust intensified so, but I couldn't break the feedback loop. The two's disgust was mine now. I felt the hate emanating from my leftmost grasp. *You hate me don't you*, I sneered at him with my mind. *I do hate you, too*, I heard back.

I made him punch himself in the face. Laughter echoed back to my ears from all of my mouths. I could hear everyone hear everyone laughing. Maybe that was the echo. The leftmost beauty laughed at the sight of his own blood on his fist; I laughed at it.

What was I doing? My drones were unhelpful blanks. It took an agonizingly long moment to recall what I was in the middle of doing. I pushed all of them to finish with the wall removal. I need space. I'm so crowded.

Chapter 9

Anna remembered staring at herself: *I still couldn't tell if I'd be up to it.* She had been the best friend I'd ever had. I avoided my reflection everywhere now. I couldn't stand to look myself in the eye. Victoria had been my shield, had respected me as much as was possible, given what she couldn't control. *There's a traitor in the mirror, and it's me.* I stared into my own eyes anyway.

I couldn't bring myself to turn away until Martin was standing behind me, waiting to talk to me, probably with something important to say. I turned away and looked into his hollow, leaden eyes instead.

"It's time, before our resolve collapses, we must confront her."

I nodded a moment before I found the resolve to speak: "I do what I must." Ill-concealed contempt washed over his face. The careful control I had noted from him of late had well and truly worn off.

"You must put a stop to the mind-controlling monster that was your friend."

"And that's what we're doing." I had to be the one to deescalate the tone again; it was a responsibility I would as soon abandon. *It's just as good that I'll soon be able to abandon it.*

"The monster will be in the safe house you used to escape us by noon. Get ready." He turned and left without even as much as another facial expression. *What do you think I'm doing right now?* I avoided my own gaze and turned around myself, leaving in the opposite direction. I left the bags under my eyes in the mirror.

I put on the expensive bulletproof vest and anti-puppeting charm. I strapped on my various weapons: the blackthorn and bone wands, the very illegal automatic, the less illegal handgun, and ammo for both. *I ask no questions and tell no lies. I know not where these came from.* I packed up the enchanted lead-lined box and lead wrapping Norah had imbued with the last of her magic. I passed the room where she left the empty pewter pentagram on top of its insulating case.

I spoke to my heart: *Please have mercy on me. Let me do what I must. I must. Let me do it.* It answered me with silence, and I walked on expecting to hear nothing, but it came through, after all. **You have no mercy for me.** My heart was fair enough.

I wondered how much, if any, of this gear would do me any good. The cottage was too small and access too constricted for any elaborate tactics. It was just in the one door, and maybe out. I could feel my destiny hovering over my shoulder, or maybe it was still Beatrice's wrathful ghost. *You want me to die with her, don't you? I'll find out if you'll get to see your wish granted soon enough.*

I sat in the car and told Norah where to turn to get to the hideout. Between directions, I recalled what I'd learned from Martin. I thought about ways to attack and block. I thought of the karate lessons I'd hated as a kid.

We finally arrived at the place, finding that as Beatrice had predicted through Norah, no one was out on guard. Norah went out towards the corpse's gulley to activate our magical defenses. I stood with Martin, uncomfortably close to the cottage I had so recently taken refuge in. There was so little left to say. We readied our weapons for the fulfillment of our non-plan.

I had the weapon I would use with untrained lack of finesse; Martin had the one that needed the benefit of his actual military training and experience. My hands drifted over my bulletproof vest to my sidearm pistol and blackthorn stick. *I hope I have enough. I hope I don't shoot myself in the foot.*

Over in the woods, I gather from what I found out later, Norah built an invocation circle with the salt of Beatrice's mummy and drew from her the power she needed for the necessary magic against Victoria's unnatural power. The cost was Norah's life. She just dropped from no known cause, at least that was the conclusion the authorities released years later. I know that her life powered the spell, and that the vengeful spirit of Beatrice had tricked her into making the sacrifice. Norah was not the kind of woman to sacrifice herself like this. I knew that much.

In the moment, it finally came time to commit to entering the cottage.
The light followed us into the place. On the inside, the wall between
the bedroom and main room had been torn out. The puppets milled
about the former main space. Victoria was back in the bedroom, with
two of her slaves at her sides. I saw her again.

Victoria stood surrounded by an army of her puppets: there was no
other way to see it. She smiled cruelly into the wall ahead of her: it
was obvious she could see us through all of their eyes. "You've come
to challenge me." She said it as a fact; Victoria knew why we had
come here. My heart settled.

"I have come to defeat victory," Martin declared, "and to avenge my
wife."

"You'll have to get through my minions first." An ugly gloating face
formed across the whole of Victoria's little gang. I swelled up with
hate for my former friend.

I resisted the urge to stroke the cast pewter charm that bound my
body to obey my mind and no other. Instead my fingers rubbed the
emptiness between them as I stared at Victoria. She looked like hell.

There was no other way to put it. Her face had hollowed out, dim and
sallow rather than shining with its usual ethereal pallor. Her hair sat
dull and unkempt. On a whole, she had the look of one who had spent
weeks doing nothing other than rotting on the sofa. It touched my
nostalgia: I remembered the summer weeks I'd spent with my sister
watching vampire media. I spared a thought for how keeping all these
minds hewn to Victoria's was affecting her; she was showing none of
my relaxed idleness.

I forced myself to focus. Martin was drifting to the right as I stood
here. The target was the mass of captured minds. I opened fire,
spraying bullets over the minions and just barely handling the
kickback. It was only a brief moment before I ran out of ammo, but
half of the puppets were down. I was dimly aware of Martin doing the
same.

I pushed forward to keep the two that had not already engaged Martin from doing so. I shot one in the back on my third attempt, just barely dodging a heavy blow from the other loose puppet. He had snuck up on me while I was focused on the one with a gun who I'd just shot while she was doing a terrible job of trying to kill Martin.

I turned away from him and promptly lost my gun to a well-placed blow to my hand. Suppressing panic, I scuttled backwards to the puppet corpse I'd just made and took her gun. I aimed with my left hand, since my right was still numb and bleeding from the blow. I shot the bludgeoning puppet in the head.

I almost laughed at the cruel absurdity as I sat on the corpse of a woman unwillingly made to serve as my old chum Victoria's human shield. I was distracted by the sound of Martin taking a hit. I screamed at Victoria, who had just buried a machete into his chest, breaking through the bar of his collarbone. She turned to the sound of my voice, and lunged at me with the bloody weapon.

Victoria's preternatural speed fuzzed her into a blur, but I shot where I knew her to be. The blade of her machete fell at a weak angle on my shoulder, glancing off without penetrating the left strap of my vest, breaking the bone underneath and slicing a shallow strip of flesh beyond the vest's protection.

I dropped the gun and awkwardly pulled her out from under her, as well as I could with my bad shoulder. Victoria should have had reflexes an order of magnitude greater than mine, but she seemed even more distracted than when she had to divide her attention between all the puppets. I had enough time to pull out the blackthorn and plunge it through her eye. Victoria had just a moment to see that I had the drop on her before it happened.

It was as if she had hesitated to bring the blade down on my head, but I had no such nicety for her. My former friend collapsed under the weight of leaden death, spilling haphazardly over the floor. I slid onto my knees next to her and flipped the body over, noticing the bullet wound in her machete-swinging shoulder, staring at her face, my bubbling rant against necessity sounding staticy and dim to my own ears.

These Final Words

I try and call out to her: I'm not dead, leave the corpse, get help, but I am incapable of speech. I breathe and bloody bubbles froth at my mouth. My reluctant comrade does not notice, she promises the corpse a lavish burial with her favourite possessions, and enough cash to set up in her ancestors' plantation in Hell, with everyone condemned that she had killed as her slaves.

I know now that as surely as I wallow in despair that I die in my time. The flesh I inhabit will decay, and God knows what will happen to my soul. I hear my ally of convenience nearby; she screamed and cradled the corpse of her friend, pleading the monster for forgiveness, telling her over and over again that she would have preferred to stop her any other way than this, and please would you look kindly on me now that you are freed from this world.

In the end, I don't believe any of it but my love mattered. Night still turns to day and day to night. As I lay trying to sleep, great heroics and evils are still being committed somewhere in the world. I am trapped in this one place, from which I look out with the only eyes I have.

I have had enough. The killer of my love is now a cold corpse, and I will soon follow.

www.ingramcontent.com/pod-product-compliance
Lightning Source LLC
Chambersburg PA
CBHW081150170626
46813CB00009B/3139